pie of flesh

edited by Zadie Smith

**consultant editor
Katie Kitamura**

First published in February 2001 by
Institute of Contemporary Arts
The Mall
London SW1Y 5AH
www.ica.org.uk

A catalogue record of this book is available from the
British Library.

ISBN 1 90030 030 3

Design: Lab Projects
Printed in England by Bookcraft

piece of flesh

introduction to this book

Zadie Smith

Hello. So here I am editing a book of five pornographic stories. Well, when I say *editing*, I mean that at the suggestion of the ICA I invited five bright, young writers with a healthy clutch of novels between them, all more or less friends of mine, to write stories of a pornographic nature for which they would receive £250 each. In effect, I paid my friends to write about sex for me. The outcome, from my point of view, is pretty fascinating primarily because, as I say, I *know* these literary reprobates and never is it more tempting to employ the age-old Western fallacy of aligning author with text than in the question of sex. For me, reading through this volume is an entirely prurient experience. For example, it never occurred to me that lovely, sweet Rebecca had sex with cab drivers or that serious Jim had a thing about Littlewoods catalogues.[1] I will look upon them all in a slightly different light now. Any invitations I may have considered extending to them w/r/t meeting my mother are hereby revoked.

But sheriouslytho: what are we to make of five of our Foremost Young British Literary Lions™ turning their pens to unworthy topics, casting their eyes to the gutter? Can we imagine such a collection coming out twenty years ago or even ten years ago? No Way José. Not at least without some openly anti-porn agenda and

---

1   Although I must admit Daren's proclivities re. canines do not come as a complete suprise.

7

more women than men in the line-up, as if the presence of women *de facto* was sufficient defence against accusations of exploitation and the aforementioned prurience. This book, in contrast, is low on nay-saying of any obvious kind, but then its contributors are of a generation for whom the saying of nays, no matter how loud and heartfelt, would be a pointless drop in the ocean against the great tide of pornography that washes over their daily lives; easy, cheap and always readily available. No amount of naying will change the fact that the average 14-year-old can get as much free porn as he or she likes, at a click,[2] without the shop and the counter, and the man behind the counter, and those funny looks. And porn is everywhere in these stories. If, again, we imagine the same collection twenty years ago, if we had asked five British writers to produce something pornographic in 1980, my guess is we could have expected stories about *sex*, about erotic things and circumstances – that is, stories about the primary situation (sex) and not its parasitic growth (porn). There is something ineffably sad about the fact that every one of these stories makes some reference to porn and the porn industry. It seems to me there are two main attitudes we can take to this.

The first attitude comes from the worst, knee-

---

2   Particularly if the 14-year-old in question is canny and heads straight for http://www.adultbuffet.com, a thoughtful gang of pornographers who search for the free pictures from the "teaser" pages of paying sites and then collect them all in one place for the 14-year-old without Visa.

jerk, right (wing) side of me; we'll call it the Sewell side of my brain. The Sewell side of my brain despairs. Despairs at this generation and its wholesale surrender to the packaging of experience, this same generation who don't say nay to the Vietnamese sweatshops that make their trainers, or the tits and ass that routinely sell their consumer durables, or the news time devoted to the marriages of Hollywood notables,[3] or the African civil wars we bankroll, or the... whatever. Too much information, as far as they're concerned. And so it goes with the porn; yes, it exploits women, and yes, it puts a tongue to the long lie of balanced sexual exchange between men and women – but it's everywhere. And in the end, it's just sex, isn't it? It's just some people having sex, no?

It would be easy to despair of a generation that feels like that. I don't think that's quite what's happening here, though, and I don't think porn wins in these stories. There is definitely a certain *leakage*, if you will pardon the term, between the porn industry and the sex of real people in real time in these stories. The other half of my brain, lets call it the Crisp side, tells me that the writers of these stories are perfectly aware of this fact and are not as young and dim as maybe you would like to paint them. Both Toby Litt[4] and James

---

3 Last night, 20/11/00. News at 10, ITV. Five minutes on Israel, *eight and a half minutes* on Michael Douglas. Yes, I know it's ITV. But *still*.
4 32

Flint,[5] for whom the title "young writer" must be wearing a little thin anyway, home in on the fetishization of the things we love to buy and the resulting sexualization of everything. I would like to write a book called **THE SEXUALIZATION OF EVERYTHING**. Don't you think somebody should?[6] Don't you think somebody should carry on where Litt and Flint have begun, and detail for us, in pure non-fictional prose, when exactly it was that we began to look for the sexual pulse in every exchange that we made; when we began to decorate our houses (as Matt Thorne notes) in such a way as to *advertise* our sexual status; when we began, exactly, to allow our sexual responses and urges – *that most primal part of ourselves* – to be packaged and *sold* back to us the same way we are shown a limited selection of vulgar sofas in a branch of DFS. In the middle of a sexual experience with a real life, real time woman, Matt Thorne's protagonist tells us the following: *"She looked up at me, and her expression seemed so open that I snapped out of porno mode and stroked the side of her face."* So when did that happen? At what point in the long slide of solipsism that is Western visual culture did our self-consciousness become so acute we became aware of such a thing as a *porno mode*? And let's be very clear by what we mean by *porno mode*. We mean: the sex

---

5 31
6 Ok, so there was Freud. But – but – actually, I can't get out of that one. There *was* Freud, and it would be Freudian of me to deny it.

we have that is an impression of the sex we've seen people who are doing an impression of the sex we have do on TV. Oh, goody.

I feel the writers in this collection have put something on the line where I have opted for the relative security of this introduction. This is not quite fair, so here goes an anecdote. The first time I had sexual contact of *any kind* I was fifteen and in my mother's kitchen. He was a ballet dancer, and as it turned out, years later, not as straight as the movies he'd been watching were telling him he should be – I'd also watched the same movies and so, equally, my sexuality had pretty much been sold to me wholesale, before I'd even so much as *touched* a piece of flesh. The result of this was that the ballet dancer kissed me rather violently on the lips against the fridge (*9½ weeks*)[7] and I immediately went down on him (*Basic Instinct*)[8]

---

[7] *9½ weeks*, 1986. Directed by Adrian Lyne. Starring: Kim Basinger, Mickey O'Rourke, Margaret Whitton, David Marguiles and Christine Baranski.

[8] *Basic Instinct*, 1992. Directed by Paul Verhoeven and Jan De Bont (you needed two people to direct that movie?). Starring: Michael Douglas, Sharon Stone, George Dzunda, and Jeanne Tripplehorn. By the by, in phoning a porno-loving friend to check on the details of these films, we got extremely confused trying to figure out the casts of these two movies, with Glenn Close's name repeatedly bouncing into the ring and complicating the issue. Of course it was Douglas who was really confusing the issue by being in both *Basic Instinct* and *Fatal Attraction*; he has much to answer for. In fact, those two movies plus *9½ Weeks* have a lot to answer for in terms of the sexual lives of a whole generation of 20-30 somethings. They inserted Michael Douglas somewhere in the dark zone between your desire and the flesh you reach out for.

without so much as a by-your-leave, and neither of us had much fun, or were able for one second to stop thinking about the *quality* of sex we were having. When I say quality I don't mean, *was it good for you, baby? Did that feel OK?* I mean quality the way McDonald's talk about *quality control*; we were thinking about whether this was the right *type* of sex, the right *style*, did it have the correct presentation, was somebody somewhere making a better burger than us [note: replace *burger* with *sex* ibid.]?

It would be nice to tell you that this feeling evaporated along with the uncertainties of adolescence. It would be nice, but it would be a lie. A misplaced dimple, the shake of a roll of fat, a stray nostril hair, all these things can still destroy pleasure for me, and not because they are unattractive but because they are a Wendy burger where I was expecting – where I have been *trained to expect* – a Big Mac. And that is a very tragic state of affairs. And these stories, funny as they are, and clever as they are, have something terribly tragic in them; they are telling us about an innocence twice taken – once in the garden, and then again, about one hundred and fifty years ago now, when the photographic image began its relentless domination of the world. Jesus, listen to the Sewell side of my brain get going again. No, no, no – it's not all bad news. We're talking women whose sexual desires are no longer sublimated into the making of quilts and other unnecessary household adornments; we're talking men who can discuss sex openly, ask what the women in their lives want and not fear the answer; we're talking relationships that include a range of sexual activities and stretch those claustrophobic roles, *masculine* and *feminine* – anyone of us, irrespective of gender, can now be the submissive, the mother, the bully, the slave. We always could be of course, but the best thing you can say about porn is that it lets you know there are *others like you*. Of course, you may be a dedicated Sewellian and of the opinion that people who like to X with a Y don't need to be introduced to yet more perverts who like to X with a Y, too. But whether you like it or not, they will find each other, and X with a Y to their hearts content, all night long.

These stories show at one and the same time the great variety of sexual fantasy and its terribly repetitive, restricted nature. From dogs to friends to underwear to sofas the fantasies are wide reaching, but the *looking*, the looking always seems the same. Look at me fucking this. Can you feel that, baby? Can you feel it? Do you want me, do you, huh, do you? It is the ugly triumph of the porn industry that it has successfully taken that most human, most vulnerable question – *Do you Want Me?* – and used it to sell everything from burgers to cars to clothes to perfume to people. Oh, yes, people. And there's the rub. The exploitation of people for the enjoyment of other people. For that, I can make no excuses for porn. No matter how many times an obscenely pumped up, plasticated, "sex-worker" on a Channel Five "documentary" tells me that her work is her "own choice" and "empowers" her, I will continue to find it a tragic way for a human being to make a living. From this point of view it seems to me that *written* porn is the most innocent variety; it harms no one, exploits nobody. It isn't subject to the awful logic of visual porn, namely, that those are real people there, in the magazine, on your desktop, suffering for their "art". Written porn is fictional and so can have no victims, right? Unless of course, porn is not a thing at all but a state of mind; unless even to write *porn* or *think* porn is to go into *porno mode*, is to let that cold financial exchange seep in to every corner of your emotional life. I hope I am not guilty of corrupting these five writers. As far as they are concerned, and to explain my hands-off editorial technique, all I can say is I paid them fairly and didn't touch them. Every word is their own.

Zadie Smith is author of *White Teeth*, which won the 2000 Guardian First Book Award, the Whitbread First Novel Award and the James Tait Black Memorial Prize for Fiction. *White Teeth* was also shortlisted for the 2000 Orange Prize. Zadie Smith is writer-in-residence at the ICA.

paying my friends for sex

Matt Thorne

Not having money was hard. But sometimes having money seems harder. It's not as if I'm rich or anything, but having enough cash to get yourself in trouble, well, you'd be surprised how quickly that becomes a burden.

I've never been an avaricious individual. Ever since I was a kid, my cash has gone on three things, and three things only: CDs, books, and the cinema. Most of my clothes were given to me; the rest come from second-hand shops. And although I spend more money on food than I used to, all this really means is these days I eat in expensive restaurants instead of McDonald's. I always eat out, and will do so until the day I die.

So when I unexpectedly started having more money, the only real evidence of my new-found wealth was in the increase of my book and CD collections. My cinema habits remained unchanged: there is, after all, only so many films you can see in a day. But although it was fun to fill out my literature and music libraries, after a while I realised there was little pleasure in buying music or books by bands or authors you didn't like. After that, I confined myself to only buying new books or CDs, or the back catalogues of bands I knew I loved. Even that got tiresome after a while (as much as I love Neil Young and Lou Reed, there's really no reason to own copies of *Landing on Water* or *Minstrel.*) This meant I needed to find some new way of enjoying my money. At first I considered developing an interest in pornography. There seemed to be hundreds of adult videos, and it seemed likely that collecting these sorts of films would give me pleasure. But after I had ten or so, I realised I didn't really enjoy pornography, and was also embarrassed about having the tapes around the house.

The same morning I chucked the cassettes away, I got a letter from an ex-girlfriend. When we'd broken up I'd been quite stern with her, telling her not to try to get in contact with me. It was over two years since we'd last seen each other, and she was writing to ask whether I would now be prepared to meet her for dinner. She made no mention of her own romantic situation, although she did say in one line that she just knew I would have a girlfriend and if I wanted I could bring her along. I hadn't thought about this ex-girlfriend that much, mainly because I had been so upset when she'd broke up with me that I'd experienced a mini-breakdown that I didn't want anyone to know about. The main reason why I had told her not to get in contact with me was because I knew she had a habit of falling back in love with her boyfriends after she'd broken up with them and I thought it was probably safer to stay away from her until I'd made a fresh start. Once I'd got back on my feet, I'd always intended to contact her, but for one reason or another I didn't get round to it, and as I've never been one for nostalgia, not having her in my life didn't really worry me.

I wrote back to her a few hours later, telling her that I didn't have a girlfriend and hadn't been involved with anyone since we split up. As I wrote this I remembered reading somewhere about how when writing love-letters you should always forget about yourself and concentrate only on arousing pleasure in the person you're addressing. I couldn't remember if the passage came from Freud or Barthes (it sounded like something from *A Lover's Discourse*, but when I checked my library this volume was missing) or someone else entirely, but I realised that this was what I was doing now, and wondered whether it was such a good idea for me to meet up with Tracey again. I had always composed my letters to please her, and felt wounded every time a reply arrived. Not because they were deliberately hurtful, but because they seemed written with no awareness of the emotions they would arouse in me, which was fine when we saw each other all the time, but more difficult during the year we spent a continent apart. The address on the top of her letter was from somewhere in Chalk Farm, so I suggested we go for dinner at The Lavender in Primrose Hill. Three days later, her reply arrived. She would be happy to meet me in the location I'd suggested.

The reason why I had been single for so long was because of a random act of kindness I had committed two years earlier. A friend of a friend had died of a heart attack at an unexpectedly early age. His girlfriend, Marianne, needed someone to look after her, and having the space and the time, I invited her to move in with me. I had expected her mourning period to last three or four months, but it showed no sign of coming to an end. Over the previous two years she had become increasingly dependent on me and although there had been nothing sexual between us, I felt too guilty to indulge in anything other than the odd one-night stand.

I arrived at the restaurant just before eight. Tracey was already waiting. She was wearing a short black dress. Smiling warmly as I entered the restaurant, she got up to embrace me.

"Tracey," I said as she hugged me, "it's so good to see you."

"You too." She looked down. "I wasn't sure if you'd come."

"So," I said, "tell me everything. Do you have a job?"

She laughed. "You're not going to believe what I do."

"Should I guess?"

"Not just yet. I have to give you some background details first."

"OK, start from the beginning. The last time I saw you, you were about to start drama school."

Tracey smiled with her head slightly tilted to one side and leaned back in her chair. It was more exciting to see her than I'd anticipated, and I was already trying to calculate how I would feel if we ended up going to bed together. The candlelight in the Lavender was doing an incredible job of bringing out all of my ex-girlfriend's most alluring features, from the small, springy, brown mole just above her soft upper lip to the exact colour of her curly brown hair. As always I was drawn in by her guilty-looking blue eyes, getting a sudden flashback of how her expression would harden when I trapped her into an argument.

"Drama school was great for the first term," she told me, "because there were so many new people and you can remember how lonely I was before we split up."

"Yeah," I replied, "I'm sorry about that."

"Sorry why?" she asked, sounding as if her question was genuine.

"Gosh, I don't know if I'm ready to get into this."

"Get into what?"

"I had a breakdown just after you left me. And although initially when it happened I wasn't able to do anything or see anyone, eventually I managed to get myself together enough to start having therapy. And through the sessions I worked out why I treated you the way I did."

I noticed from the direction Tracey's eyes were pointing that a waitress had come across to our table. I felt glad of the interruption, amazed that I'd started talking about this stuff so quickly. Then I remembered how my therapist had spent our final session trying to convince me that I wouldn't feel properly healed until I'd seen Tracey again, and how adamant I'd been that that wasn't a good idea.

The waitress told us the specials and we looked up to the blackboard to decide what we wanted. I guessed from Tracey's small order that she was having money problems. While not wanting to embarrass her, I attempted to persuade her to have more than just a starter by letting her know that I'd pay.

"It's OK," she told me, "I'm really not that hungry. But if you order a nice bottle of wine I'd be happy to drink it."

I ordered the wine and my food, then said,

"I feel terrible now, isolating you like that. But it wasn't jealousy. I always thought it was jealousy, but my therapist made me realise it wasn't that at all. I just needed to get something from you, something secret, something from inside, something you probably couldn't give. That's why I took us away from everyone else."

She nodded. "I do understand, and that's kind of why I wanted to see you. You see, like I said, drama school was great for the first term, but then I started missing you. And I looked back on our time together with a fondness you'd never believe. Every day I thanked God that we'd had those two whole years together so I had something from every season to remind me of you. Like, pick a day..."

"Hallowe'en."

"Scary badger."

"What?"

"You remember."

I thought about it and realised that I did. We'd gone to the cinema together and on the way back we'd seen two liberal-type parents trick-or-treating with a small child wearing a cardboard badger mask. And we'd joked with each other about how the parents would've convinced their child he didn't want to be anything as horrible as a hobgoblin or Freddy Krueger. "No," we imagined the two well-meaning parents saying to their child, "what you want to be is a scary… badger."

I smiled. "I find it hard to remember stuff."

"I know. When we broke up you said you'd never think of me again."

"I didn't say that."

"You did."

"Well, it wasn't true. So, are you going to tell me what your job is?"

"Phone-sex."

"Huh?"

"I knew you'd like that. Can I tell you about my audition?"

"For the job?"

"Yeah."

"OK."

"Well, I'd been working for TicketMaster for a while and it just wasn't working out. The rest of the people in the office didn't like me because every now and again I'd have an audition for an advert and they'd all get really upset because I had a life outside work. So, anyway, there was one woman there who I became work-friends with, and one day she told me she was leaving. She'd got a job working for a sex-line and it was five times as much money for nowhere near as much work. I was a bit sceptical, but she told me that although there were a few dodgy men at the company, the main people in charge were all women, and by that time the little pound signs were dancing in front of my eyes and I'd agreed to go in for an interview."

The waitress reappeared at my elbow with the

wine and the squid salad I'd ordered for a starter. I asked her what had happened to Tracey's food and she said she'd thought it would be better to bring it at the same time as my main course. Tracey nodded and said that was fine. I still felt guilty about ordering so much food when she was having hardly anything and tried to make up for it by overfilling her glass with wine.

Tracy continued. "So I went in for my interview and found myself in this windowless room with two women and one man. Although the man did most of the talking, it was obvious from the outset that the women were in charge. Anyway, my audition consisted of three exercises. The first two exercises were pieces I had to read from a script. This is quite a long anecdote, but the punchline's in the middle instead of the end so get ready to laugh. The script I was reading from was supposed to be as if I was talking from the perspective of a woman who had been led into sexual ruin. I had to go through this catalogue of things that my boyfriend had made me do and the twist at the end was that I had tell the caller that I was now completely cock-crazy and even just knowing there was a man on the other end listening to my past exploits got me off. The script was kind of torturous and confused and I was trying to understand it as well as read it so I kept stumbling over my words, and I got to this bit where I said my boyfriend introduced me to swimming and just as I was thinking that was odd and waiting for some sub-aqua exploits, the men stood up and shouted at me, 'it's swinging, not swimming. My boyfriend introduced me to *swinging*."

It wasn't that great a line – she knew that – but the delivery was so perfectly Tracey that it made me laugh, identify with her and feel horny all at the same time. I knew one day lots of men would share this feeling, and it was this knowledge that made me certain that in spite of Tracey's considerable fragility, she would one day achieve success as an actress.

She went on. "The second script was less interesting. Standard sexy housewife, naughty knickers stuff. But then the final exercise was an improvisation. It'd been a while since I'd been to a proper audition and you know how much I like that sort of thing anyway so I got all overexcited and started acting as if I was auditioning for a movie instead of a job on a sex-line. You would have liked the scenario though. It was a bit close to home and I could tell they'd come up with this idea for an audition piece deliberately to make me feel uncomfortable so I decided to take it to a real extreme. I was supposed to be an actress who'd come for an audition for a part in a film and then when I'd arrived I'd found out it was actually a porno instead of a normal movie."

I popped a large piece of squid into my mouth and started chewing. Tracey brushed a strand of stray hair out of her face and carefully lifted her overfilled wine glass to her lips. As she did so, I noticed her lipstick was completely the wrong shade for her, making it look as if she'd been sucking gob-stoppers all day long.

"The weird thing about this last exercise was

that they wanted me to do it over the phone. I suppose it wasn't that weird, given that I was meant to be proving I could do a sex-line job, but the way they handled it was odd. First off the women came across and hooked me up to a headset, then the guy went off into another room on his own.

"Like I said, from the moment I was told what the exercise was I felt really irritated and wanted to embarrass them, so I tried to make what I was saying as disturbing as possible, telling him that I was only taking this job to support my baby, and that I came from a really religious background, and had wanted to be an actress my whole life, grown up on *The Kids From Fame*, stuff like that . . ."

"How did he respond?"

"Well, that was it, after I'd been talking a couple of minutes or so he stopped asking me questions and just kept saying 'go on, go on,' and I could hear the clink of his belt and, y'know, I knew what he was doing."

"What did you do?"

"What could I do? I kept talking, but I tried to make it sound as unsexy as possible, just praying he would stop. But he kept going and I kept going until he came."

"Ugh."

"I know. And the worst thing was he didn't even try to hide it. I think I probably could've handled the situation if he was just some pervert doing this job as a sneaky way of getting his rocks off, but he came back into the main room with his fly undone, shirt-tail still sticking out, and the two women looked at him and made another mark on their clipboards as if this was just another test I'd passed."

"Tracey," I said gently.

"Yes?"

"How long have you had this job?"

"Only a couple of months. It's alright once you get used to it. And I make it fun, playing little games with myself like working out which words will make them . . . " She looked at me. "Oh dear. When I imagined telling you about this I thought it would make me sound glamorous and sexy."

Not wanting her to worry, I smiled at Tracey and let my fork drop back on my plate.

We stayed in the restaurant until eleven. By that time we were both a little drunk and I was reluctant for the evening to end. I felt more aroused than I had in months and didn't want to go back to the sexless friendship waiting for me at home. So I persuaded Tracey to walk down to a nearby pub for one final drink. The front of the pub was crowded so we went through to the back bar, which was empty except for an old man and a fruit machine. I bought us both Stellas and sat opposite Tracey. Her legs were crossed at the ankles and I found myself staring at the line where the hem of her dress pulled tightly around her toned thighs. She was telling me about a friend's play but I had long stopped listening to her words. Taking a large gulp from my drink, I swooped in on her, sliding my hand up under her skirt.

My fingers stopped as they reached the soft crotch of her knickers. My lips stopped as I realised they were pressing against a resistant mouth.

"I'm sorry," she said, with tears in her eyes, "I don't want to do this."

When I was sixteen I went on a school-organised trip to Keele University. The trip was designed to introduce potential students to college life, and given the excesses of this weekend away, I think the organisers managed an accurate distillation of most people's three-year experience. I was the only one my school expected to make it to university, so I went alone, although by the end of the coach journey up I had befriended a sizeable number of sixth-formers sent by other schools in the city. As my school was ridiculously suburban, a haven of bubble perms and teenage pregnancies, I had always been an outsider, so much so that the first years started a rumour that I slept in a coffin. I didn't go into school that much, spending most of my time in my bedroom listening to the Pixies and those first three Ride EPs. This was considered so outré in my neighbourhood that I was amazed to find that my tastes were shared not only by the sixth formers I'd befriended on the bus, but also the students who organised the last night's disco.

Those two days at Keele were, to that point, the best of my life. But as I returned to my isolation, I saw no likelihood of them ever being repeated. My parents were both intensely anti-social people, ashamed of their marriage and quick to discourage me from forming friendships with others. But my new-found comrades were reluctant to let me disappear back to my previous existence, bombarding me with calls until I agreed to come with them to a Primal Scream concert. I went with them, and over the next few weeks, found myself with my first ever social circle.

And after friendship came the inevitable romantic infatuation. Among my new gang was a beautiful redhead with goth tendencies and a tart sense of humour. The rest of my friends were dubious about some of her more extreme tastes, and I was the only one willing to accompany her to a Cranes concert at a local polytechnic. The show was terrible but the night was transcendental, and in the taxi home I tried to kiss her. She stiffened, pushed me away, and said she wasn't interested. As far as I could remember, I'd never told Tracey about this, but it was definitely a formative moment, making me overcautious in the opening stages of any subsequent relationship. If I got any sense that the woman I wanted didn't want me, I immediately backed off, even if their reluctance was only part of an elaborate flirtation. In some ways, I'd never really got over that first rejection, and now the same thing was happening to me again, I felt a fresh desperation. But that doesn't explain what I said next.

"Tracey?"

"Yes?"

"I'll give you five hundred pounds to fuck me."

During the taxi ride home, I wondered whether I

regretted making my offer. There was no question that Tracey had been horrified, turning me down immediately and remaining upset until we said goodbye, but when I thought back to my sessions with my therapist, I realised the fact that Tracey would never want to see me again was probably a positive thing. My therapist had never accepted my excuse that I couldn't start another relationship because I was giving house-space to Marianne, trying to make me believe it was really because I held out hope that Tracey and I would get back together. Now that definitely wouldn't happen, I was free to get on with my new life.

Marianne was waiting for me when I got home, sitting in front of our television drinking a mug of mulled wine and watching a film featuring Veronica Lake. She moved her legs down so I could sit next to her. As usual, her eyes were rimmed with red and she'd dressed with the bare minimum of effort. I squeezed her hand and she flashed me a brief smile.

The following morning I went out with three female friends of mine. Hazel, Ivy and Elizabeth were all young, recently married mothers. I had met them through Marianne. Initially, they had been her friends, calling me up for news about how she was coping. But as she hadn't seen them in two years and they had stopped asking about her, I now considered them my friends, meeting with them once a week for a few hours of coffee and chat in a cafe in St. John's Wood.

Every now and again, we were joined by the unofficial fifth member of our party. Her name was Anita and she was by far the most glamorous member of our quintet. Marianne would've been furious if she'd known Anita occasionally accompanied us, as Anita had supplied Marianne's boyfriend Donald with the drugs she believed had precipitated his premature heart attack. Anita had been having a low-key affair with Donald for several years, and Marianne blamed herself for being so understanding about her infidelity, knowing that if she'd been more possessive she might've saved his life. Donald was one of many men Anita had spent years seeing on the side, although she usually went for men of more considerable means. Between affairs, she was always short of money, lost without someone to pay for her.

Hazel, Ivy and Elizabeth were all fascinated by the fact that I had been single for so long. Ivy was the only one who flirted with me, although I knew this didn't count for anything, as she was as certain in her marriage as the others. But they couldn't understand why I didn't make a move on Anita. Every time the subject came up, I used the same excuse,

"Marianne would kill me."

"But how would she know?" This was Elizabeth, the most persistent of my three friends.

"She'd know. She'd smell it on me."

"I don't see why you're worried about that," said Ivy, sucking her lip. "You've let Marianne live with you rent-free for two years. She's in no position to tell you who you can sleep with."

"There's too many demons."

"Between you and Anita?" Elizabeth asked. "Why? You hardly knew Donald. Besides, you two have an incredible chemistry. I bet the sex would be amazing."

"I don't think so."

"Why not?"

"I get the impression that Anita can keep people at a distance even when she's fucking them. I hate having sex with someone who's got their barriers up."

"You only say that because you've heard how she talks about her businessmen blokes. It'd be different for you. You'd be able to break her down." The other two chuckled darkly at this, encouraging Ivy to add, "If I had your body I could do it."

I sipped my coffee and took a bite from my Russian cake, feeling unsettled. I still wasn't really over last night and felt less comfortable bantering than I usually did. I knew myself well enough to know what I really needed was sexual reassurance and although, in a strange sort of way, that was what my friends were trying to offer me, thinking about Anita made me uneasy.

"Let's talk about something else."

That evening, I went to a party with my bank manager. She was one of the normal girls who'd made my life so difficult at school. We'd become friends by chance when

I went into my hometown bank to open a third account. She'd been impressed by the amount of money I'd been depositing and asked me out on a date. We'd quickly discovered that there were the same differences between us now that there'd been at school, and we'd gone home separately. This had been a big blow to me as she'd been one of the most unobtainable girls in my school, and having spent a large part of my adolescence masturbating with her in my head, I was keen to see whether the real deal rivalled the fantasy.

After our unsuccessful date, we had concentrated on forming a workable business relationship. I needed more from my bank manager than most people, and was on the phone to her several times a week. And once long enough had elapsed for us not to be embarrassed in each other's company, we started going out together as friends. I became her walker, accompanying Vicki to social events once or twice a month. These events were not grand affairs, consisting mainly of nights in the pub or dinner-parties organised by her friends.

Tonight's party was in Jamie's Bar in Charlotte Street. One of Vicki's friends had just returned from two years in Australia and a gathering had been organised to welcome him back. Vicki didn't seem that excited about the party, and unusually for her, wasn't even worried about changing for the evening, meeting me straight from work. Seeing her in a conservative suit reminded me of how great she used to look in her school uniform, and I wondered again about my impotent reaction to the women in my life. It was odd: I was excellent with strangers, no matter how attractive, able to go into a club or bar, find someone single, and persuade them to take me home with them. But as soon as it came to anyone with whom I had the slightest emotional connection, I became a complete drip.

Feeling depressed, I drank too much and found myself telling Vicki what had happened with Tracey. I made a joke out of it, saying that it was probably not a good idea for me to tell my bank manager I'd been offering ex-girlfriends extravagant amounts of money for them to sleep with me.

She downed her glass, winked at me, and said, "I could do with some money."

We went to her place. In the taxi we bartered about the price: Vicki saying she wanted twice the amount I'd offered my girlfriend; me saying for that much money I expected something special.

I wasn't that surprised by the way she reacted. Vicki had spent the whole of her adult life working with money, and no doubt saw this as a neat way of mocking its black magic. The idea of being paid for sex clearly appealed to her, as did taking a human transaction so lightly. I paid the driver and we went into her house.

"So," she asked, "how do you want me?"

I thought back to all those adolescent afternoons. My fantasy had always been that while I was masturbating about Vicki she was somewhere masturbating about me. I told her this, thinking that was maybe how we'd start.

She chuckled. "You know I never did. Not about you. I must've done it about almost every boy in the class, but never about you."

I couldn't reply. She noticed my sadness and said hurriedly,

"I would've done, though, you know, if I'd known you were doing it about me."

"You must've known."

"Why?"

"Every boy in the year used to masturbate about you. We used to compare experiences."

She looked at me. "Really? I honestly had no idea. Can I tell you about a fantasy of mine?"

"Of course."

"I used to fantasise about groups of boys in the class masturbating over me. You know, with all that AIDS talk in assemblies sperm was seen as such an evil substance. But it didn't seem that way to me. I wanted to be totally coated in it."

She must've noticed my horrified expression, as she immediately eased back from our sexual conversation and asked me instead if I wanted a coffee. I nodded and she went out into the kitchen to make me one. I took advantage of the spare moment to assess my surroundings. Houses always look strange when there's only one person living in them, but Vicki had done a good job of making her place look comfortable. Before Marianne moved in with me, there had always been something defiant about my decoration, as if I was

35

trying to create a home that would be the envy of anyone who visited it. But nothing I could buy from a shop could add the warmth created by another person's belongings.

Vicki was clearly less troubled by being alone, and although she couldn't quite disguise the fact that she had too much space to herself, the lounge looked like somewhere she'd be equally happy entertaining friends or watching television alone. I liked the fact that she'd left stuff out (a hairdryer lying on its side next to a rectangular white extension-plug; a box-set of *Friends* episodes by the television; three cotton-wool balls dyed scarlet with nail-varnish on a copy of the *Express* next to the electric fire), and began to relax as I settled down into her settee.

She returned with my cup of coffee. After her revelations about her childhood cum-fantasies, I didn't feel like watching her masturbate any more, and anyway, that was far too passive. It was time for me to become masterful.

"Take your trousers off," I told her.

"Let's see the money first."

"What?"

"Cash up front. I don't want you changing your mind after you've had me and pretending the payment thing was just a joke."

"OK. How much did we agree on?"

"A thousand. Do you carry that kind of money with you?"

"No. Will you take a cheque? You know I'm

good for it."

"Do you have your cheque-book on you?"

"No, but come on, Vicki, you're my bank manager. You can easily debit my account whenever you want."

"Write me an IOU."

"I don't have a pen."

"There's one on the table."

I got up and wrote out an IOU, wondering what was behind this banter. Although a thousand pounds wasn't bad for one night's work, I couldn't believe that Vicki was genuinely only doing this for the money. The way I looked at it, the play with potential prostitution was just spice to stoke up enough excitement to get us through a one-night stand. If she was taking it seriously . . . well, fuck it, if she was taking it seriously, I'd just make sure I got my money's worth.

"Right. Now get those trousers off."

She stood up, walked across to the table and checked the IOU. Seemingly satisfied, Vicki came across to me and put one foot up between my legs.

"Unbuckle my shoes first."

I felt pleased she was bossing me back, thinking that this proved she was getting into what we were doing. I gripped her ankle before following her instruction, a motion that seemed to please her. Shoes removed, she turned her back to me. I sunk down slightly so her bottom was directly in front of my face, then waited as she undid the buckle on her belt and slowly lowered her trousers over her buttocks. She was wearing a flimsy pair of white translucent knickers: the kind that pulled tight between her legs so that the material covering her bum formed a triangle. I gripped her hips. She let her trousers fall to the floor and stepped out of them.

"I bet you're a man who likes bottoms."

I giggled. "What?"

"Let's see, shall we? What happens when I do this?"

She slid her fingers under the elastic of her knickers and pulled them down. Using a foot to flip them onto a pile with her trousers, she leaned forward and pushed her bum up in my face, using her fingers to pull open her cheeks. The light was good in Vicki's apartment and I had a full view of the soft creases of her anus. She was right: I did like this sight, although few of the girls I'd been out with had shown it to me so readily, and it was a hard thing to request of a one-night stand. I could see why Vicki was so willing to reveal hers to me. I know this sounds strange, but it was absolutely beautiful, the skin moving so perfectly to the small hole in the centre with each tuck in exactly the right place. From this angle I could also see a rear view of her vagina, which was equally well defined, the flesh of her outer labia almost spookily symmetrical. Vicki seemed to revel in my slow appraisal and after my nice, long look I pushed my tongue onto her welcoming folds. I held Vicki's hips and managed to get deep into her, curious whether she liked having this done to her as much as I liked having it done to me. I licked for a while and then asked her,

"Can you touch yourself while I do this to you?"

"Well, I can, but you'll have to hold me open."

"That's OK."

She released her buttocks and I took over, opening her even wider. The muscles in my tongue felt pleasurably strained as I buried my mouth into her bottom, wanting her to feel totally loose. She fingered herself slowly at first, but when I showed no sign of wearying she speeded up. I wondered if she would be prepared to come with me and felt scared about how much I wanted that to happen. But I also wanted to come too, and as her moans grew shallower I stopped sucking her asshole.

"What's wrong?" she asked.

"Nothing. I realise it's not very romantic to interrupt the sex like this, but seeing as I'm paying…"

"Yes?" she asked, impatient.

"What are you like with orgasms? Do you come? Can you come? Do you always need fingers, or can you come just from fucking? Can you come lots of times or is it one-time-only, lights out?"

"I'm weird. Back to front. When I masturbate it takes forever, but I guarantee if you fuck me for more than three minutes that'll hit the spot."

"That's not back to front, that's perfect. And can you still fuck after you've come?"

"Yeah, but if we're gonna do that can we use lubricant? You don't have to wear a condom."

"Of course. Have you got some?"

"I'll fetch it."

She moved away from me and went out into the hallway. I watched her go, finding it sexy to see her bare legs beneath the jacket of the work-suit she was still wearing. I waited while she went upstairs, rubbing my cock through the pocket of my trousers. When Vicki returned she could tell I was looking at her cunt and stopped beneath the main light, letting me see her. As I'd expected, she had a neat bikini line, an unnecessary precaution for one so fair, but nice to look at all the same. Although this was definitely an incredibly sexy moment for me, I couldn't help feeling slightly disappointed. *Seeing Vicki Wade's cunt…* this was a childhood dream come true, but how could it hold the same magic for me now that it had done back then? I remembered one time when a boy from our school had told us that he'd seen Vicki doing stretches in the gym, and her leotard had ridden up so high that, as he'd put it, 'he even saw her pin.' For months afterward I'd dreamt about being in his place, even (if you'd caught me in a weak moment) prepared to give up my life to share the sight.

Maybe I should've offered her money back then. She probably wouldn't have accepted it, but who knows? Of course, in those days I couldn't even get near her, let alone start a conversation that would lead up to me offering her money to show me her cunt. It's odd, but even now, the thought of Vicki's adolescent vagina tucked inside that unfaithful leotard seemed sexier than the reality in front of me. I'm not a pervert, and have no

40

interest in schoolgirls (even women my age dressed up in school uniform), but the power of that missed moment was so strong that the fantasy almost managed to obliterate what was happening now.

Vicki seemed to notice my distraction and brushed her fingers down over herself. She pretended that she too was distracted, but then quickly looked back at me and smiled when she saw me grip myself through my trousers again.

"What do you want me to do?"

"I want to come inside you."

"I've already said that's fine."

"I know, but I need to be sucked first."

"Oh, OK." She walked back to me, knelt down and unzipped my fly. Pulling open my trousers, she slid my cock out through the slit in my boxer shorts and took it into her mouth. I don't really need to describe the experience other than to tell you she was good at it, although to be honest I've never been with a woman who wasn't. Remembering her promise of how little sex she needed to orgasm, I let her suck me longer than I normally would, eventually stopping her with a gentle pat on both shoulders.

She looked up at me, and her expression seemed so open that I snapped out of porno mode and stroked the side of her face. She bent down, unlaced my shoes, and stripped me from the waist downwards. Picking up her blue tube of lubricant, she squeezed a blob onto her palm, spread it over my cock then rubbed the rest inside her. Pulling my cock forward, she slid herself gently on top of me. I kissed her, realising as I did so that it was the first time our lips had touched. It's embarrassing and inappropriate, but the first time I fuck someone I always want to tell them I love them. Thankfully, tonight I conquered that urge and mouthed it softly to myself instead. Our fucking was surprisingly (for me, anyway) forceful: a proper, deep, heterosexual shag that carried us both to orgasm and left us woozily clinging to each other. We stayed like that until Vicki climbed off of me and asked,

"Did you get your money's worth?"

Marianne was asleep in front of the television when I got back. She often nodded out in the lounge, waking up again about three or four and going to bed. Feeling bolder than usual, I decided to carry her upstairs. When we reached the landing she awoke, and after taking a few seconds to adjust to the situation, sniffed my neck.

"You smell of sex."

I didn't say anything. She smiled, and let me carry her to her room and drop her on her bed. As I turned out her light she said,

"Someone called for you. There's a message on the machine."

I went downstairs and played the message. It was Tracey, apologising for the other night and saying she wanted to see me again. Tomorrow. Although it was after one, I called her straight back. She reminded me of her address and told me to come over at seven o'clock. I replaced the receiver and went to bed.

The following morning Marianne and I both awoke earlier than usual and decided to have breakfast together. This was quite an unusual occurrence for both of us, and as we lacked even the most basic supplies, I headed off to the deli. When I came back Marianne had made me a coffee and was sitting at the end of the table sipping hers, wrapped in a dark-blue silk dressing-gown.

"So," she said, as I hunted for a grapefruit-knife, "who was the lucky girl?"

"On the phone?"

"No… last night."

"Oh. My bank manager."

"Really?" She laughed. "I thought you were too rich to have to sleep with someone for a raised overdraft."

"I was. Until someone started eating me out of house and home."

She looked at me, clearly shocked. I'd never referred to money before, and she'd stopped bringing it up after her third straight week of thanking me for my generosity.

"I do feel ready to start looking for a job," she said in a small voice, "although if it's alright with you I'd rather stay here and pay you rent than move out. I'm just so comfortable here."

I didn't answer, preparing her grapefruit in silence and placing it in a bowl in front of her.

I arrived at Tracey's house an hour and a half late. This was a deliberate tactic, my childish way of getting revenge for her knocking me back after our previous date. She pretended she wasn't aware of the time, greeting me with a hug. Feeling optimistic, I'd stopped off at an ATM on the way and taken cash out of each of my three main accounts, now having nearly a thousand pounds on me. It was good to feel my ex-girlfriend's body against mine and I clung onto her until she broke away.

"Would you like a drink?" she asked. "I have beer. Or whisky."

"Beer, please."

She fetched a bottle from the kitchen and handed it to me. Tracey had already strategically placed an opener on the coffee table and I used it to uncap the drink.

"Aren't you having anything?"

"I will in a minute. I already had a little too much this afternoon."

I could tell she was nervous. Tracey was not a casual drinker, and when we'd been going out together she had only drunk at home at moments of extreme emotion.

"Are you OK, Tracey?"

"I'm fine," she replied, sitting on her sofa.

She was wearing a cream cardigan, a white halter-neck and a short grey skirt. Tracey had always had a thing for flesh-coloured stockings, and was wearing a pair this evening, with no shoes. I sipped my beer, waiting to hear why she had summoned me here.

"The offer you made the other night."

"Yes?"

"Does it still stand?"

"Of course."

"What if I don't want to have sex with you?"

I wasn't in the mood for this sort of game playing, and wasn't about to beg. I put down my beer and stood up. "Then I don't think you should."

"No," she said, looking up at me, "I don't mean that. Oh God…" She rubbed her forehead. "What if I want to do other things?"

I sat back down. "What sort of other things?"

"Safer things."

"I can wear a condom."

"I don't mean that sort of safe. I mean, emotionally safe."

"I'm not sure I follow."

"Well," she said, "would you want to see me?"

I smiled. "Of course. But let's not make this so clinical. Why don't you come over here with me?"

"But how will we work out the money?"

"The money doesn't matter to me. How about if I give you five hundred pounds anyway, and then you can decide how far you want to go?"

"And you won't get angry with me?"

"Of course not. Don't be stupid."

"Or tell anyone. Or hold it against me?"

"I don't know anyone you know. And it's my idea. How can I hold it against you?"

She still didn't seem satisfied. I was beginning to wonder if this was such a good idea, but was feeling too turned-on to leave.

"And you accept that this will be a one-off? You won't force me to do it again later because I agreed to it now?"

I couldn't understand why she was being like this. Throughout our relationship I had almost always been the submissive one, never forcing her to do anything. I might have been a little more forthcoming than her about my desires, but that'd only been because she rarely talked about what she wanted, preferring to go unhappy than verbalise her discontent.

"Tracey, I'm not about to cast judgement on you. I offered you money the other night because I was desperate to sleep with you and couldn't cope with being rejected. I can understand why you were offended..."

"I wasn't offended, just scared. I'm frightened by you wanting me."

"Why? You work on a sex-line. You have men wanting you all the time."

I realised the moment I said this that it was a mistake. Suddenly, everything became clear to me and I saw my way out of this. But first I had to listen to her response.

"Jesse, this is why I got so upset the other night. I told you about the sex-line because I thought you'd find it sexy and funny, but I didn't think it would change the way you thought about me. After I said it I remembered how afraid I was about telling you about my sexuality. This is something I've been wanting to tell you for ages, in fact, that's the whole reason why I got in touch with you again. But then at dinner you told me you'd had a breakdown and I couldn't tell you the truth... well, I mean, I told you part of the truth, about how I missed you and was glad we had all that time together, but I couldn't get to the heart of it. I couldn't tell you... look, you know what you said about your therapist telling you that what you were feeling with me, when you isolated us, wasn't jealousy but you wanting something from me, something I couldn't give?"

"Of course."

"Well, you and your therapist got it completely round the wrong way. What you wanted was to know the truth about me, but because you were so jealous you didn't want to hear it."

What she was saying made sense. I thought back to my bank manager telling me about her cum-fantasy and how that hadn't turned me on at all. I had often told Tracey I wanted to know what she masturbated about – and in my head I thought I did – but the truth was, if she wasn't doing it about me I didn't want to know.

"The truth is, the reason I freaked out the other night was because it felt like you were making the offer out of anger. And it reminded me of how you always used to view sex as something you had to take from me, as if I was deliberately withholding it. That 'something I couldn't give' was an honest sexual response, because

I always felt you were judging me.

"But the thing is, I do want to do something with you. Something that'll get rid of all the hurt and make you think well of me. And although it sounds strange, and it did upset me at first, I think you paying me for sex is a good idea. Only you have to be doing it for pure motives. You have to do it because you want me."

"I do want you."

"Good." She came across and sat next to me. Taking control, she straddled me and pushed me back on the sofa. She'd washed her hair recently and I could smell her shampoo as her long brunette curls fell over her face. As she started kissing me, I considered how this evening's experience was already so different from my previous night with Vicki. I had completely forgotten how Tracey kissed, the soft pulling that felt so reassuring after her resistance in the bar after the restaurant, and as I let her take charge, I found myself thinking back to when I first got my money and was trying to develop an interest in pornography. Although it had quickly stopped working for me, it was only now that I realised why. It was my lack of imagination, and my inability to bring details from my own life into my appreciation of the films. My one-night stands were few and far between, and to be honest, they weren't fantasy-occasions, instead usually arising from desperation and mutual need. And although I've always had lots of women in my life, it's been hard to eroticise them, as I've known them as friends rather than sex-objects (I realise the two are by no means mutually exclusive, but until last night with Vicki, it'd always seemed that way to me). So when I watched pornography, I found it hard to enjoy the variety, which I guess is the whole point in the first place. It was difficult to identify with the well-built men, and unless the women looked like Tracey, or other ex-girlfriends, they didn't seem sexy either. I'm not a natural voyeur, and watching other people having sex always makes me feel like I'm the one being exploited, not them, as if I'm stuck in someone's house and still having to be the polite guest even when my hosts start going down on each other.

Now that I was having sex with Tracey so soon after I'd had sex with Vicki, and was rediscovering myself as a sexual person (albeit in quite an unconventional way), I felt like I might like to watch pornography again, using the woman on screen as a point of connection between Tracey and Vicki and whomever I ended up having sex with next.

I was amazed at how much the money was adding an extra energy. When I'd been going out with Tracey, our intercourse had always been extremely fraught, a cycle of tears, excitement, pain, pleasure and tears. The first few times had been terrifying, a form of lovemaking I was completely unused to, having previously only been with women who saw sex as a friendly adult kinship. Now I was paying Tracey she seemed to be trying to fit her need around working out how to make me happy. The way she was kissing me showed she wanted me, which is something I've always needed to know in order to enjoy sex with anyone. These last two statements sounds antithetical. Let me explain. What I mean is, nothing is as big a turn-off for me as a woman saying, 'I want to make you happy.' But a woman who wants me (even if she's only pretending) is all I need for the sex to work. This is why I always aimed low when picking people up, and why paying my friends for sex was turning out to be so successful. I'm not vain enough to imagine I could sexually excite a professional prostitute, but I also knew that it would be impossible for a friend (or an ex) to have sex with me without feeling something. And with Tracey I thought it went much further than that, as I saw now that she'd always needed this sort of excuse to really enjoy sex, and may even previously have had this sort of fantasy herself.

She stopped kissing me and pushed herself up. "How much would you pay to pull down my top?"

"I told you. I'll give you five hundred pounds whatever we end up doing."

She shook her head. "No," she said, "I want to negotiate."

"OK," I smiled, "I guess that could be fun. Are you wearing a bra?"

Tracey got up and pulled her curtains. Then she turned on a table lamp and switched off the main light. Before retaking her position on top of me, she pulled off her cardigan and hung it over the back of a chair.

"Yes, I'm wearing a bra."

"So you're only talking about me seeing your bra, not your breasts?"

"For the moment, yes."

"And let me get this straight, am I paying you to pull down your top yourself or for me to do it."

"Either."

"So there's no price difference between those two options?"

"No. Come on, how much?"

"Well, it seems quite minor, so let's say ten pounds."

"Twenty. I take it you have the money with you?"

I felt surprised that Tracey was being as serious about the money as Vicki had been yesterday, especially as I'd assumed I'd have to persuade her to take the cash. But I enjoyed my role in the fantasy, taking a twenty-pound note from my inside pocket and laying it out on the table.

"OK," she said, fingers going to the thin cord around her neck.

I reached up and stopped her, saying, "No, I want to do it."

I untied her and pulled the top down over her breasts. She was wearing a white strapless bra and her nipples were visible through the material. I attempted to stroke them.

"No, no," she told me, "you haven't paid for that yet. How much to see my knickers?"

"What type are you wearing?"

"Does that affect the price?"

"No, I'm just curious."

"Mnn," she said, "you just reminded me of

something."

"Dinner in the oven?"

"No. A memory. From when we were together."

"Dangerous territory."

"Doesn't have to be. Anyway, this is a nice memory. It was about the third or fourth time we slept together, and we met unexpectedly, or maybe I hadn't been planning to go to bed with you but it ended up happening anyway, and you were surprised because I wasn't wearing matching underwear and I felt really weird because I didn't even have that many matching sets and you'd already seen most of them."

"So you're not wearing matching underwear today?"

"I am, actually, although I didn't think about that this morning. Well, kind of matching, they're white string-knickers, with a small red design in one corner."

"Let me see."

"How much?"

"Forty."

"Cash on the table."

I unfolded another two notes. "Are you sure you don't want me to give you the whole five hundred right now?"

"And spoil the fun? I'm enjoying myself, aren't you?"

"Of course."

"Good." She smiled at me and pulled her skirt up. She tried to make the material stay as high up her thighs as possible so I could get a proper look at her knickers. Shortly after we'd started going out, I'd discovered Tracey's diary. Just before we'd started going out she'd had a lonely night with some unsatisfactory ex-partner and come home and detailed all the things she liked and didn't like. Eventually I was forced to admit my betrayal of her trust, but prior to my confession it provided a useful shorthand on how to please her. She liked having her breasts caressed rather than kissed, preferred having her knickers gently slipped down her thighs rather than taking them off herself, sometimes enjoyed being fingered to orgasm with her knickers still on, although that was never quite as nice as being eaten out. She liked sucking cock; sometimes more than being fucked. Her favourite fantasy was imaginary incest (something only ever exciting to those who hadn't suffered the irritation of real-life siblings) and except for very, very rare occasions, hated being on top.

She laughed. "I bet you're just dying to touch me, aren't you?"

Tracey never used to be this confident. I knew it had something to do with the money, but I also thought it was probably connected to her new job. I'd always known Tracey had the perfect voice for sex-line work, but felt surprised that she'd actually gone through with it. I wanted to ask her more about what the job was like, but after her previous outburst, felt scared about spoiling the mood.

"Can I touch your cunt and breasts at the same time?"

"If you're prepared to pay for it."

"I'll give you fifty pounds. But you also have to rub my cock."

"For fifty, I'll only do it through your trousers."

"That's all I want, for the minute." I counted out the cash and put it on the table. "Although let me touch you for a bit first."

"OK. Can I lie back more?"

"Of course. It'll make things easier."

She shuffled backwards, reclining against the arm of the sofa. I moved round between her legs, leaning in to kiss her as I began to gently stroke and squeeze her breasts. Her kisses were more open now, her mouth more relaxed. I quickly embraced her and then began to rub the heel of my hand over her cunt. I touched her breasts at the same time, kissing her again. After a few minutes, she pushed me back up and began stroking the tight crotch of my trousers. She stroked her hand around my shape, the heel of her hand rubbing my cock while her fingers softly dug against the underside of my balls. I let her do this for a short while, then pushed her back.

"Another fifty to see your tits."

She laughed. "Shall I undo it?"

"No, let me."

I put a fifty-pound note on the table, and Tracey leaned forward to let me unhook her bra. I was amazed at how unfamiliar her breasts looked, and wondered how I could've forgotten something so important. Why are visual memories the hardest to preserve? Especially sexual memories. I couldn't believe that in my fantasy-world I had robbed Tracey of her real body and replaced it with an anonymous alternative. I had forgotten how easily she flushed; that her shoulders were lightly freckled. Her breasts had become bigger in my memory, her nipples smaller, and the real-life combination was much sexier. But strangest of all, I had forgotten how Tracey looked at me differently when I started to undress her.

She kissed me. "Knickers too?"

"Let me do it. You know what you said earlier about not wanting to have sex with me, do you still feel like that?"

"I don't want to have penetrative sex. But everything else is OK."

I considered this. "Alright, then I'll give you a hundred and fifty pounds to pull your knickers off and go down on you."

"OK."

Placing the cash on the table, I gently lifted Tracey from the sofa and brought her down onto the floor. She raised her knees and I slipped my fingers under the waistband of her knickers and gently tugged them down. Her cunt was already wet and slightly open, the pink bright beneath the spring of her light brown pubic hair. I pulled her legs slightly more open and gave her cunt a first kiss. She murmured something and I moved up to hear what she said.

"What was that?"

"I said I've fantasised so much about you doing

this. Especially since the other night."

Remembering Vicki, I asked, "What did you do when you fantasised?"

"Touched myself of course," she said, sounding surprised.

I couldn't stop myself asking, "When was the last time?"

She sounded slightly irritated as she replied, "In the shower at the gym this morning," and not wanting to push my luck, I went back down on her.

It was incredible to be between Tracey's legs again, and I felt disappointed when she came quickly. I wanted to carry on and see if I could bring her to a second orgasm, but she stopped me and made me come up alongside her for a hug. We lay like that for a while and then I asked her,

"Would you like to see my cock?"

"Do I have to pay you?"

"No," I laughed, "it's a freebie."

I pulled open my fly. She looked at me, surprised.

"You wear underwear now?"

"Since Michael Hutchence died."

"Show me then."

I pulled out my cock. She stared at it for a minute and then looked up at me.

"I remember it."

"Do you?" I asked, surprised. "Exactly?"

"Exactly."

I looked at her, wondering if women's memories

worked differently to men's, or whether the fault lay solely with me.

"So," I said, "two hundred quid for a blow-job."

"It's extra to come in my mouth."

"Two fifty then."

I counted out the cash and she went down on me.

Marianne was already in bed when I got home. I knew she was probably still upset about what I'd said that morning, but found I didn't really regret it. Since I'd started paying people for sex, my generosity to her had started to seem unfathomable, and I couldn't understand why I'd been kind to her for so long. No one else seemed interested in her (in the whole time she'd lived with me she'd never mentioned her parents once) and she hardly contributed anything around the home. Besides, if it wasn't for her living here I could have my sexual adventures without venturing outside the front door. I wasn't quite ready to kick her out, but from now on I felt she should start doing something to justify her board.

I didn't have much to do the next day. I arose late, masturbated, then went out for lunch alone. When I got back Marianne was sitting in the garden, reading a book. I went through to my study and called Vicki.

"Hi, Jesse, how are you?"

"Good."

There was a moment of silence. I hadn't

imagined that it'd be hard to talk to her, assuming that we'd quickly fall back into a friendly intimacy, maybe with a pleasant new sexual undercurrent to our conversation. But suddenly I was experiencing the same sort of shyness I usually only felt when I was talking to someone I really fancied.

"Is this a money conversation?"

"Kind of," I laughed.

"Oh," she said, "I'm glad you've brought that up. The thing is, Jesse, the other night and everything I did enjoy it, but I don't think it should happen again."

"Really?" I replied, wondering if she was serious, or just wanted to be persuaded.

"Yeah," she said, "I'm sorry. I can't really explain. It's not you, or the money. It's just that I'm not very good at the stage between casual sex and a proper relationship, and I know you're not looking for that right now…"

"Well…"

"I mean, I'm not either, and I want you to carry on being my walker, and well, if I'm going to be absolutely honest the next day I was a bit freaked out by the fact that I'd taken money from you and if you'll let me I'd like to give it back."

"No, Vicki, don't be silly, it was worth it."

"I don't have to give you the actual money. If you want I can just credit your account."

"No," I said, "I'm glad I paid you. But I understand why you don't want to do it again, and don't worry, this won't damage our friendship."

"Oh good," she replied, "thanks, Jesse."

I finished the call, found my address book and flipped through until I found Anita's number. I dialled, and got her ansaphone. So I tried her mobile.

"Hello?" she said, the background noise of a lively pub behind her voice.

"Hi, Anita, it's Jesse."

"Hi, Jesse, how are you?"

"Good. Where are you?"

"In Soho. Why?"

"Are you alone?"

"Yeah. Why?"

"I wondered whether I could meet up with you."

"Now?"

"Is that OK?"

"Of course. I'm in Waxy's Little Sister. Do you know where that is?"

"No."

"Opposite the Metro."

"The cinema?"

"Yeah. How long are you going to be?"

"About forty-five minutes."

"OK. I'll see you then."

I told Marianne I was going out and took a taxi into Soho. Part of me wanted to reveal that I was meeting Anita, just to see how she'd react. But I worried that giving Marianne clues as to what I had planned might inhibit me, so I kept quiet.

During the drive, I thought about Anita and wondered whether she would go for my suggestion. The fact that she was drinking alone in the afternoon seemed a good sign, as she only lapsed back into alcoholism between affairs, focusing more heavily on drugs when she was involved with someone.

I remembered talking about Anita with Hazel, Ivy and Elizabeth, and how they were convinced I'd be able to seduce her. It was almost worth not using the money as a motivation, but I realised when I thought about having sex with Anita the financial transaction was the part I was looking forward to most. It was knowing that I was going to offer Anita money that stopped me feeling intimidated by her, as it seemed more adult, honest and decadent than her booze, coke and affairs.

Waxy's Little Sister was a ghastly Irish theme-pub, and I couldn't understand what Anita was doing there. She was sitting alone with a pint and a small glass of whisky. I walked across and joined her.

"Hi, Jesse. So what's wrong? Is this to do with Marianne?"

"No, nothing like that. I was just at a loose end and wanting someone to have a drink with. You were the first person who came to mind. Well, second, after my bank manager."

She chuckled. "Isn't he working?"

"She. And yes she is. But I thought I could persuade her to knock off early. Anyway, I'm glad you were free. Are you alright for drinks?"

She nodded. I got myself a pint and pulled up a chair beside her. Even when she was getting wasted alone Anita looked incredible. She looked posh and innocent, a fatal combination even without the added spice of her exciting private life. I'd always wanted her, but had been held back by fear. Her red hair (always a warning sign to me, since that first experience of adolescent rejection) made her look a little like Nicole Kidman at her most elegant, although with a slightly more inviting, open face.

"How are you then?" I asked, still nervous.

"Alright. Starting to get a little bit wobbly. How about you?"

"OK… a little drained."

"Ennui?" she smiled.

"Something like that. Too much money and too much free time."

"I wish I had that worry."

I sipped my beer, sensing an opening. "You're alright for money, aren't you?"

"Are you kidding? I'm broke. I've never had this little money in my life."

"Really?" I said, and after enough large swallows, began my pitch.

The following evening I was feeling lonely again. I couldn't get hold of Anita, or Tracey, and knew it would be undignified to have another go at persuading Vicki to change her mind. Frustrated, I went downstairs to the lounge.

Marianne was lying on the floor, watching television. She was wearing a short skirt and a black top and when I sat on the sofa behind her I could see her knickers. She paid no attention to me, concentrating on the television. I stayed there for fifteen minutes, but finally couldn't take it any longer and asked,

"How much money would you want to suck my cock?"

Marianne moved out the following morning. I would've been happy if she'd left the night before, but she clearly wanted to drag out her departure. I wasn't sad to see her go, and although I had said some seriously mean things to her in our argument the night before, none of my comments had been unfair. Two years of frustration had come out too fast, that's all. I wasn't a bad person.

"I think it's good that you kicked Marianne out," Elizabeth told me, "she's been sponging off of you for far too long."

"What was the argument about?" asked Hazel.

"Never mind that," Ivy interrupted, "what I want to know is, what is Anita like in bed?"

I answered both their questions, at length, by telling them the story of my past week. This time I definitely wasn't trying to reel anyone in, knowing that all three of my friends were happily married mothers who weren't short of money and liked to think of themselves as decent, moral individuals.

Ivy was the first to start turning the conversation. Her approach was obvious, getting me to repeat the concept over and over again ("So, let me get this straight. You've been paying your friends for sex?" "Yes, Ivy, that's right, I've been paying my friends for sex") until it no longer sounded outrageous and they'd all accepted it as an acceptable thing to do. But Hazel was the one who made it personal.

"Would you pay me for sex?" she asked.

"Would you like to have sex with me?"

"Maybe. How much money are we talking about?"

"Well, I paid Vicki a thousand, Tracey somewhere around five hundred and Anita two-fifty."

"You paid Anita the least amount of money?" Ivy exclaimed, shocked.

I smiled, amused by her indignation. "I asked all three of them to name their price. Anita wanted two-fifty."

"That's terrible," said Elizabeth, "she must have such low self-esteem."

"How much would you want to sleep with Jesse?" Ivy asked Elizabeth.

"Definitely a thousand," she said, "at the very least."

It was fun checking into a hotel with three women. We went to The Tenderloin, a tacky rock themed hotel that Ivy claimed was the only place for an afternoon assignation. I was shocked by her knowledge and wondered whether I'd been right to think of these women as being so innocent after all.

We took the lift up to the third floor and found our room. I could tell the three women were enjoying themselves, although I thought it probably had less to do with the sex than the fact that we were all doing something secretive together. They always got like this whenever we left the café, even on the most innocent of missions. I think it was because we were moving outside the expected limits of our friendship, and none of us had the emotional maturity to cope with that.

Ivy took off her shoes and jumped backwards onto the bed. She was the shortest of my prospective partners, although none of them was tall.

"So how are we going to do this?" asked Hazel. "Are you up to having sex with all three of us?"

"Not in a straight way."

Elizabeth looked worried. "I'm not doing any lesbian stuff."

I laughed.

"I mean, not that I don't like you both and everything," she said to Ivy and Hazel, "I just don't think I could bear it."

"I'm not sure about the masturbation part either," Ivy admitted, "I don't even do that in front of my husband."

"What is it that embarrasses you?" I asked. "Doing it in front of me or doing it in front of each other?"

"Each other," they agreed.

"Cause I could call down to reception for three blindfolds. They do do that sort of thing here, don't they?"

"They do," Ivy admitted, "there's an S&M bag they give to favoured customers."

"What do you think?" I asked them.

"I'd still be embarrassed," said Elizabeth, "even with only you watching."

"I don't mind doing it," Hazel told me, "as long as you do get the blindfolds."

"Ivy?"

"Oh God, honestly, Jesse, I don't think I'd even enjoy it. Can't you just fuck me?"

"Well, I will, but I wanted us all to do something together."

"Ok, how about if I strip down to my underwear and watch you having sex with Elizabeth while Hazel masturbates?"

"But Hazel doesn't want you to see her masturbating."

"And I don't want you to watch Jesse having sex with me," added Elizabeth.

Sighing, I decided to cut my losses. Ivy would wait in the bathroom, Hazel would masturbate, I would fuck Elizabeth. The women would all wear blindfolds. I worried that this would turn the afternoon into a slapstick comedy, but they were adamant. We moved everything they might bump into and called reception, who sent up a boy with three blindfolds on a silver tray.

I asked if anyone wanted to undress before I

blindfolded them, but they all wanted to stay fully clothed to begin with. Their anxieties had made me feel uncomfortable and I began to wonder whether this was such a good idea. But even if we stopped now our friendship would still be changed forever, and in spite of everything, this was still a sexual experience I wanted to have.

"You are going to wear a condom, aren't you?" asked Ivy.

"And not the same one," Hazel added, "a different one for each of us."

"I don't have any," I said.

We called reception and they sent the boy back with a packet of extra-safe Mates. Ivy went out into the bathroom and closed the door. Hazel took off her shoes. Elizabeth lay on the bed. She whispered to me that she wanted me to undress her, so I took her shoes off and unbuttoned her jeans. I felt most worried about having sex with Elizabeth and was trying to make sure the experience didn't feel inappropriately intimate. I pulled off her jeans. She was wearing simple, pale cream knickers. I removed them quickly and looked up at her face, watching her breathing as I went down on her, again trying to make the sex feel as straightforward and competent as possible.

I was paying so much attention to Elizabeth that I hadn't even had chance to look at Hazel, who was probably the one of the three I was most excited about going to bed with. I gently nuzzled and kissed Elizabeth's clit, reaching up under her jumper and pulling the cups of her bra down from her large breasts. Behind me I had heard Hazel getting out of her dress, but she was managing to masturbate without making almost any sound at all.

I continued sucking Elizabeth, realising my only real opportunity to look back at Hazel without Elizabeth sensing it was during the few moments it would take me to move from licking her cunt to fucking her. After that I could probably get another couple of glimpses but would have to really strain my neck. I would've sucked Elizabeth for longer, but I was so eager to see Hazel that the moment I thought Elizabeth was wet enough to fuck, I stopped and turned round. Hazel was wearing a long stripy top that together with her hand almost entirely obscured my view of her cunt, but her facial expression and the quick movement of her finger suggested that she had got over her embarrassment of masturbating in front of me.

I turned back from her, fixed my condom and slid my hard cock into Elizabeth's cunt. She was wet, but it did take a couple of thrusts before I was moving smoothly inside her. Seeing Hazel like that made me excited again, and I worried I wouldn't be able to last long enough to satisfy all three women. Elizabeth had been avoiding kissing me, so I didn't force it, gratified when I felt her hands holding my hips.

I didn't want to get Elizabeth too close and then stop, as I knew that would prove frustrating to her. I also didn't know where she was going to go when I swapped over to Hazel. In the bathroom with Ivy, I guess. I slowed down, and Elizabeth nodded, seemingly happy for me to stop. I pulled out of her, and helped her get dressed and go into the bathroom. The moment the bathroom door closed, I walked over and snogged Hazel. She seemed perfectly happy to kiss me, wrapping her arms around me and reaching for my cock.

"Hang on," I said, "I've just got to get rid of the condom."

"Forget the condom. Just get rid of it and fuck me."

She reached up and untied the blindfold. I snapped off the condom and lifted her off the chair, pushing my cock into her as I pressed her against the wall. She grabbed my hair and we started fucking furiously, finding a satisfactory position somewhere between standing and a crouch. We continued like that until I said,

"I'm sorry, I'm getting close. And I've got to stay hard for Ivy."

"Can't you come twice?"

"Not usually."

"OK. Go down on me then. I'm pretty close too."

She lay back on the bed and I gave her head until she came. Afterwards, she squirmed and reached for my hand. I kissed her and we stayed on the bed until Hazel called out to Ivy,

"He's all yours."

"Come in here then," she called back.

"No, don't worry, I'm going down to the bar."

Hazel dressed and left the room. Ivy walked in, still blindfolded. I let her come towards me. She gave a short, dirty laugh as her fingers reached my chest.

"Come on, then, what have you got left for me?"

I felt vaguely irritated at Ivy for stopping me from properly satisfying Hazel, and for the way she had always previously been so flirtatious with me, but then joined in with Elizabeth's squeamishness when it actually came down to us all getting together. So I went down on her until her fingers were digging into my head, then fingered her as I fucked her from behind, making her come just before I emptied myself into her.

That was the last I saw of Elizabeth, Hazel and Ivy. They never contacted me again, and didn't return my calls or e-mails. Anita and I met once more for sex, but then she got involved with someone else and said she couldn't see me any more. Tracey, too, seemed to have decided against further meetings with me, and although Vicki was happy to talk to me about money, there was no chance of anything sexual happening between us. At first I was glad to be free of Marianne, happy to have the house to myself, but it didn't take me long to become lonely. And with no friends left, there was no possibility of pursuing my previous path. I lasted two weeks before I started buying pornographic videos again, watching them with a hunger I had never had previously. And when they stopped working I found myself in a phone-box, intending to try Tracey again, but after getting halfway through her number, stopping and dialling the digits on a small colour card in front of me, finally ready to begin the next stage of my existence.

Matt Thorne is author of *Tourist*, *Eight Minutes Idle* and *Dreaming of Strangers*. He is also co-editor, with Nicholas Blincoe, of *All Hail the New Puritans*.

"legends of porn"

of

porn"

(polly morphous): final shooting script

Toby Litt

Lee Perverse and Polly Morphous first met on the set of the Kurt Spurt/Wolfgang Bang VeryHardCorps ~~film~~ production, 'Hey, Guys, It Just Stopped Hurting XIV'.

[We open on an empty soundstage. Narrator (tbc) walks leonine towards camera, wearing sharp acrylic junglewear.]

Back then, Lee was working under the name 'Sodeep Sodark' and Polly was known only as 'Extra, If Needed'.

'Hey, Guys,...' was Polly's first porno and Lee's fiftieth. But, between them, on this very soundstage, something clicked – and what happened afterwards, well, that was *sexual* history...

[Cut to archive footage – baby-photos, Yearbook-photos, amateur-photos.]

From the very start, their lives were parallel. Born poor, raised hard - their only way out from the tough streets of San Francisco was through the sex industry.

[Cut to Narrator, on the tough neon-lit streets of SF.]

Lee started off hustling outside local motels and diners; Polly got a very bad reputation in school, and was able to trade it up for a pole-dancing gig and what is ~~euphemistically~~ laughingly called 'a modelling career'...

[Fade in on poolside interview.]

It was Kurt Spurt who spotted the star quality in both of them:

"Obviously, you know, it's not easy to see

whether someone is really going to get the viewers hot - I mean *really* hot. In order to make that diagnosis, you gotta see them in action - up close, up *real* close. I could see from the moment he unzipped his jeans that Lee was enormously gifted. But it was only when he took with so much gusto to the *submissive* role that I knew I had someone I could take to the top - and over it."

[Cut to Narrator, ~~still~~ back on the soundstage.]

Kurt is lavish, too, with his praise of Polly:

[Cut to Kurt, on the tough neon-lit streets of SF.]

"When she walked on-set, even though the production guys have seen a *lot* of flesh, they were begging straight off for bit parts. She had something about her – a kind of innocence; something that guys really wanted to destroy. She didn't *look* like a pornstar, not the old kind. I don't think a surgeon had been *near* her body. It was as if she'd somehow evolved into being just *totally* desirable. I knew the *moment* I saw her that I had to team her up with Lee."

And team up they did.

[Cut to VT, 'Hey, Guys, It Just Stopped Hurting XIV' – hall scene.]

During their first half hour together, nothing spectacular happened.

Wolfgang Bang, who was producing, recalls:

[Fade in on corner office interview, swingchair.]

"We weren't worried about Lee, you know. He could handle himself. He had it down. Never had a problem with Lee. Not one. But Polly had to prove herself. If you watch it now, even with a professional eye, there isn't much in that first scene in the hall to tell you that erotic magic is about to happen. Lee has all the chops. Polly comes across as a bit of a screamer. Let's face it, she's a first-timer and she's trying too hard. Lee should look like he's in control, and he doesn't. Kurt called 'Cut', he and I sat down, talked it through. He'd seen Polly eyeing-up the couch when she came in. He figured, Hey, she might have something about doing it on couches. We decided to give her another chance, this time… on the couch."

[Cut to Narrator, sitting on "The Most Famous Couch in Porn" – in the Museum of Porn, Washington DC.]

Little did either of them know at the time, but this was to be the most important decision either of them ever made.

As Kurt said, afterwards, "I just had an instinct.' And what an instinct it was…

[Cut to 'Hey, Guys, It Just Stopped Hurting XIV' – couch scene.]

The scene started normally enough. Lee and Polly enter the room. They are already naked, having moved through from the hall. Seated on the couch are Ursula Undress and The Rabbi. She holds his cock in her hands, but nothing much is going on. ~~As the Rabbi has been part of the series since 'Hey, Guys, It Just Stopped Hurting IX' there is no explanation of his presence.~~ The scene develops as one would expect, right up till the moment Kurt gives Polly the direction - edited out in the released version, but here dubbed back in:

"Give me more! Improvise! Come on! I want something special!"

You can see the moment of ~~puzzlement~~ doubt on Polly's face.

[Close-up, repeat, slow-motion.]

What can she possibly do that she isn't already doing?

Then she, too, has her moment of inspiration:

"Wow, I *really* like your *couch*. Where did you get it?"

The other actors react in various ways, but their professional skills allow them to carry on, just.

Lee glances off-screen, towards Kurt.

[Close-up, repeat, slow-motion.]

[Voice over. Kurt, mumbling.]

"I could tell that Lee wanted to know whether he should go with this. I think I just shrugged."

The Rabbi raises his eyes momentarily towards heaven.

[Close-up, repeat, slow-motion.]

And Ursula Undress, being somewhat distracted anyhow, seems not to be taking it in.

[Close-up, repeat, slow-motion.]

[Cut to archive footage of Lee and Polly.]

[Interviewer, off-screen, asks them:]

"Lee, what did you think, that first time Polly mentioned the couch?"

"Well, to be honest, I hadn't really noticed the couch before… "

[They laugh – Polly punches Lee playfully in

the upper arm.]

"No, but seriously… this was the first time anyone had really seriously challenged me to act while I was doing anal. What I came to see later was the aspect that Polly was trying to push the whole thing further, take it to another level. I had to think fast. *Did* I like the couch? Where *had* I got it from? And so I said… "

[Cut to 'Hey, Guys,…. XIV']

"It's new. I only bought it yesterday."

[Cut back to archive footage. Polly says:]

"And so I say… "

[Cut to 'Hey, Guys,… XIV']

"You have reallly good taste. I love this couch. It's so soft and leathery-smooth against my skin."

[Cut to Kurt Spurt, outside a dive bar, ~~looking shifty – the man wants a drink, *bad*~~.]

"Man, from that moment on, the whole thing just went wild. Everyone got in on the act. For the rest of the scene, they did all the usual stuff, oral, anal, double. But the whole while, they kept talking about the couch, the decor, the colour scheme… I can't deny, I was a bit *freaked*. I mean, how's this going to play? I could see the sound-guy snickering. But I've always been open to new things; and there was something really *fresh* about this, something real."

[Cut to 'Hey, Guys,… XIV'. The couch scene runs to the end.]

Rabbi: "I noticed it, too. It's really good quality."

Ursula: "I have a couch just like this at home."

Polly: "Perhaps we could go there some time."

Lee: "What a great idea."

Polly: "How did you get the idea to combine the pale leather with the pink throw cushions."

Lee: "I've always had a certain visual flair."

Ursula: "You can say that again."

Rabbi: "I only wish I was so gifted."

Polly: "What kind of couch do you have, Rabbi?"

Rabbi: "Nothing special."

Ursula: "Hey, maybe we could all go down the couch store later and pick him something out?"

Lee, Polly, together: "That's such a *great* idea!"

Rabbi: "Well, I mean, if you'd really like to."

Lee: "We'd *love* to."

[Cut to Wolfgang Bang, driving a golf cart.]

"To this day I can remember the atmosphere on set when that scene finished. Everyone there was just stunned. What we'd seen was… I don't really know how to put it. It was the breakthrough everyone had been looking for."

[Cut to Narrator.]

"Now housed in the Museum of Porn, Washington DC, this couch has become the single most visited item in the entire history of the sex industry. For on this couch, a pivotal moment took place. As Wolfgang Bang explains…"

[Cut to Wolfgang Bang, piloting his Lear Jet.]

"We couldn't do much with that scene in 'Hey,

Guys… XIV'. The script had already been written. We were on a tight schedule. And, besides, we needed to see what kind of a reaction it got. But we started work on a sequel straight away - that night, even. Kurt and I went to my beachfront place, sat right down, and started typing out a scenario. That scenario became the first Polly Morphous / Lee Perverse flick, 'Trying to find a decent couch for the Rabbi.' We finished at about five in the morning. Right away, we knew that what we had in our hands was a paradigm shift. We went out for a walk on the beach, smoking some fine Cuban cigars. It was like, History. We knew we could relax. Then 'Hey, Guys… XIV' came out, and was such a massive success - our biggest film to that point. We'd been sitting on the script of the Rabbi's couch, but now we put it forward into production. Unfortunately, in between times, the original Rabbi had died of a massive heroin overdose, so we had to replace him. That wasn't too difficult. We'd always needed an understudy on hand, anyhow. The shoot went really smoothly. We hired a store one night and just took it over. By this time we'd come up with the idea for Polly and Lee's names. Everything just went click. You could hear it. Everyone could hear it. With that click, an entire industry began to quake."

[Cut to 'Looking for a decent couch for the Rabbi'. Wolfgang continues in voiceover.]

"I mean, look, for a start, none of the actors took their clothes off for the entire first forty minutes of the film. That was unheard of. Instead, we just let them improvise. We got a handheld camera and followed them throughout the store. Polly was totally in control. She lead us from couch to couch. And when we got there, she'd get everyone to sit down on it and describe how comfortable it felt. She had a wonderful natural gift for scenic construction. The film built from a fairly plain cotton-covered couch in pink to a slightly larger more showy one, then to the tigerskin, the white leather and finally the calfskin - which was, of course, the most expensive. The Rabbi got more and more excited about how his new couch was going to look when he got it home to his apartment. We wrapped that day's shooting late in the evening. The following day, we had moved the couch (the calfskin one) onto the set that was meant to be The Rabbi's bachelor pad. And I have to say, it looked fantastic there. We shot the final ten minutes straight off, just as they stand. It was wild. There'd been so much foreplay, without it being really foreplay. All the actors were just frantic. It was so real. *And*, of course, we ended on that famous final line…"

[Cut to 'Looking for a decent couch for the Rabbi':]

The Rabbi: "Jesus, I love this couch!"

[Cut to the Narrator, browsing in a porn superstore. He looks up, as if surprised to see us there. But he's relaxed. Hey, he's not ashamed to be seen buying hardcore. He's that kind of a guy. He picks a copy of 'Couch I' off of the shelf.]

"'Looking for a decent couch for the Rabbi' went on to become first the biggest selling movie in VeryHardCorps' history and then the biggest selling movie in the history of the entire porn industry. What happened afterwards has become a legend. The Polly Morphous/Lee Perverse became the most successful syndication imaginable. And throughout the industry sexual acts were relegated, for the first time, to a ~~subsidiary~~ minor role in porn movies."

[Cut to Kurt Spurt, in a bar, drinking.]

"We couldn't make them fast enough to satisfy the demand. After 'Looking for a decent couch for the Rabbi' we did 'Looking for a decent rug to match the Rabbi's couch' and then 'Looking for a decent couch for the Priest' and then 'The Rabbi and the Priest move in together' and then Couch films for the Imam, the Krishnas… Then we did a bunch, which were Polly's idea. 'Polly Morphous and Lee Perverse Go Shopping for Curtains'. It was money all the way. Perhaps we should have paid more attention to who was making us that money."

[Cut to the Narrator, walking through an idyllic graveyard.]

"The lives of porn stars are short, fast and often end in violence."

[A gravestone comes into view.]

"That of Polly Morphous was shorter and faster than most, but her death – at least - was perhaps as she would have wanted it."

[Cut to Kurt, in the same bar, later – ~~he looks bad~~.]

"Polly always loved the ocean. When she got a little money, the first thing she did was invest in scuba lessons. After the films hit big, she got a huge schooner-boat, and a private dive-coach. She was on at us all the time to do 'Polly Morphous and Lee Perverse Swim with Dolphins'. One day… she pushed it too far. She wasn't experienced enough. She went down too deep. I think that was her problem all along: she always went too deep. Man, I miss her."

[The Narrator stands in front of the gravestone. We see the inscription. 'Polly Morphous/Swimming towards the light/ Constantly'. He looks towards us, moved.]

"Everyone who knew her said that Polly was a pure soul, too good for this world."

[The Narrator turns away from the grave, and begins to walk towards the sea.]

"Lee Perverse left the porn industry soon after Polly's death, and has not returned. Although the two stars will always be thought of in the same breath, there was never a hint of off-screen romance. Lee rapidly made another fortune, in the discount soft furnishings industry. L.P. Stores are a feature of every Californian mall, and there are plans to take the franchise nation-wide."

[The camera pans round to gaze towards the glistening ocean.]

"But one can't help but wonder, how often does Lee Perverse think of the lost spirit that was Polly Morphous?"

[We close in on a dolphin, cutting nimbly through the surf.]

[Titles. Sad music. Out.]

Toby Litt is author of *Adventures in Capitalism, Beatniks* and *Corpsing*. His forthcoming novel *deadkidsongs* will be published in February 2001

porno-
graphic
story

Rebecca
Ray

I'm not lying now. I'm going to tell you this story and you have to listen, you have to listen close. Because I've waited a long time for a story like this one to tell. Alright? This story is pornographic, you have to listen closely and you have to believe. Just to enjoy it, you have to suck the whole thing out of reality, you see? You turn the lights out to watch one on television, so the shadows only flicker over silhouettes in your room. It's like that. It's the story of how I fucked a cab driver at two o'clock in the afternoon, parked up in the archway between Air Street and Regent Street, Piccadilly Circus end.

I love London, loved it from the first day. London's full of people like pornography's full of sex. I thought that, the first day. I used to sit in this café on Charing Cross Road, watch the people walk past. And they never meet your eyes and you never meet theirs, but they're walking to be watched. They know you're sitting there, they feel you like the softest touch on the side of their face. They wet their lips and smell the exhaust fumes, and they know you're sitting there. They feel the contours of their own features, their own body under their clothes, all the more clearly for your eyes. They feel themselves. London's full of people, full of fingering glances and sounds. A man told me once, touching my stomach in bedroom light, that my body was a landscape: a jungle and mountains, desert. All bodies are like landscapes maybe, with a city for the mind.

London's full of fantasy, people come here and

they leave their names behind. My boyfriend, he grew up here, he doesn't feel it maybe. But I've never felt it as strongly as I did that afternoon. Air Street is this little passage, right? It runs you from Regent Street into Soho, from one side of London to the other in the moment it takes you to pass under the arch. That's how close the two sides are: silk gloved fingers and dirty fingers, interlinked and gripping tight. Does that sound stupid? Does it sound right? When it rains, the water pushes trickling fingers between Air Street's broken paving stones, under the arch and out. Into Regent Street's bright sky. Into its open road. London is everything, it's the pornographer, it's the audience, and it just breathes with being them. Full of fantasy, and never more so maybe, than when you open a black cab's door. You could be anyone then. You could be a princess then, you could be spending stolen five-pound notes. Or you could be ten minutes away from fucking a man whose name isn't given to you. London allows fantasy, needs it like a camera trained on people without clothes.

We love each other, London and I. I could put my hands down on the street and grey my skin with it. I could stand in its centre, my eyes closed, and feel every sound and every movement like things I've always needed to feel. I came here, I left my name behind. I never went home again. And, parked up under that archway in Air Street, we fucked that day, London and I.

A November day, it was, the sort that blows people and litter before it like it doesn't care which it moves. The sort that bruises every face. And this is how it happened: on Embankment, me standing there with my arm stuck out and no idea, no idea. I saw the cab slow, standing there. Cold air and breath and traffic fumes, caught in the river wind. I was going home.

This guy, he was early thirties maybe, dark hair and brown eyes. He poked his tongue into his cheek, looking up at me, like he didn't give a fuck if I was beautiful or ugly, didn't give a fuck where I was coming from. Like I shouldn't expect him to. They like to talk, cabbies, but they only talk through the glass and they don't look back at your face. And I talk, and it's London I'm looking at. There's something very free, I think, something absolute, in speaking to a stranger without ever meeting their eyes. He had brows that almost met in the middle, this guy. He had a wife, two sons and a daughter, he told me. He had a life, somewhere else. He asked me if I was going home.

"Home, yes," I said. On the other side of the glass, I saw him nod. "My boyfriend'll have the kettle on by now."

"That's the best thing, isn't it. That's what you need, cup of tea when you get in. Just sit down with someone for a bit." He told me that he didn't like to talk when he got in. He just liked to sit with her, relax without having to talk. He told me, sometimes the talking gets on top of you, doing that job. Always having to talk. And one of the best things about being married was that you could sit in silence, without coldness, without awkwardness.

"I could never get married." I looked out through the window: Embankment and the shadow of the footbridge, moving over us. People moving, everything moving, like the wind could rattle and shake every person in London, and no one would ever come loose. "I'm not the right sort of person."

He told me that you didn't have to be any kind of person to get married. Marriage, he said, was a good thing for anyone. I looked at him, his neck, his shirt collar, and my reflection was painted across the glass, in shadow.

"I don't know. You get married, you'd have to be the same person every day. I mean, you wake up, he's the same... he makes you the same." I looked away from his back, and I said, "He'll have the kettle on when I get in now, but we're not like that, see? You get married, you're always the same."

"No, it's not anything like that. Everyone changes. You spend a few years with someone, both of you are going to change, aren't you. Try having kids. No, I mean, my wife, she's a completely different person from the one I married. Totally different, like. But she's still the same underneath. Anyway," he said, "you've got a boyfriend, just the same with a boyfriend."

"I came home, a couple of months ago, I'd just got paid. You know what I said to him? I said, 'Let's go to the airport.' And you know what he said? He said yes. We went to Rome that weekend. You get married, you don't do things like that anymore." I looked at his eyes in the rearview mirror. "How's she different then?" I said. "How's she changed?"

"Lots of ways. I don't know, lots of ways. Got a different job, hasn't she? Different friends."

"What does she do?" I said, "Your wife." And London was going past us in low gear. I listened to him answer and then I said, "My boyfriend, he's got a different job every six months, and we're always skint. And you know what? I don't care. I don't give a fuck. Because he's never the same, week to week. But that's not it anyway, it's not that they're always the same. It's that they make you the same." I looked at him. "You know?"

"I know what you mean. Course I know what you mean, but –"

"See, you do have to be the right sort of person for marriage. I couldn't handle that. I couldn't be the same person every day, you know? That's what I love about London," I said. "You can put on your makeup and clothes and be someone different, any time you want to, any moment, you know? You can walk out the door and meet somebody and be a different person." I met his eyes then, and we were smiling at each other, but I couldn't see his mouth. "I like that," I said. "I like to have that, you know?"

∗She imagined the sort of wife he would have. She imagined his wife reaching up, the tiniest touch with the tip of one finger, where his brows met in the middle. His eyes would be closed, she thought.∗

Through the glass, I could see his arms moving. And we were turning now, and all the grey streets turning too. He stopped to let a woman go past. In London's winter, people move as if they can't stop for the wind. And I saw her look in through the windscreen, maybe she saw me. I met her eyes.

We were eight minutes from Air Street then. He had dark hair, just like his eyebrows, thin on the back of his neck.

I said, "How old are your kids?"

I've never found people attractive by their faces or bodies. The look of someone is a blank thing, dust on a TV screen. It's the way that someone wets the corner of their mouth, it's what's in their eyes when they take you in, and you can imagine the sound they might make as they come. It's the way that they would hear your sounds, and feel the need to move, hearing them. The smallest things, do you know what I mean? I want you to know.

I watched him answer. And outside: Londoners walking. Londoners, brushing against each other, and feeling the touches without a flicker of expression. The engine ground as hard as the wind out there, through Charing Cross and onto Haymarket, filthy grey.

No one here seems to look at each other. No one needs to look, everyone knows that it might break the spell. Everyone in London walks as though they're walking alone, but they can only keep that expression because of the people by their sides. This place, it scrapes people against each other, until they could crackle and scream.

You have to believe in London to love it, like

you have to believe in pornography so you can let it make you come.

I said, "I couldn't do it, marriage, children. I have to able to get up in the morning and know, I can do anything I want to do." I saw his shoulders move, shrugging. On the glass between us, my reflection was still. "It's playing," I said. "That's what it is. It's the best kind of playing in the world, to pretend, to do something really new, you know? To do something mad. I'm the sort of person, I couldn't live without that."

∗She imagined how he'd sit with his kids, how he'd go home to them. She imagined them on the sofa, crowding round him, all grabbing for a little piece. He would look out over them, trying to find the television screen with his eyes.∗

I said, "How do you live, without that?"

Coming up to Piccadilly Circus then, where every street spits people onto the road and lets them press together there.

I said, "When was the last time you did something mad?"

∗She imagined the flickers of anger on his face, trying to find that television screen, the way his hands would push them away. And on the screen, she could imagine it, people fucking. She could see how it would be.∗

Here on Piccadilly Circus, with every person pushing dryly against each other, I can see it all: Soho's ragged edge. The clean, tall shops. The traffic. The sky. Here, this is where I'd stand and close my eyes. This is where I'd put my hands down onto the pavement and let them come up grey. There is a noise here, there is a feeling. Do you know the feeling where everything strains? Back arched, muscles tensed, and eyes closed like that, everything in your landscape body tries, everything in your city mind. London is the fantasy; it shows you what you want in every window, in the reflections sliding over every car; it gives you everything that you want to believe in. It gives you yourself.

I said, "When was the last time? Something you've never done before? Something that was nothing like you at all?" He had big hands, I could see them on the wheel in that grey afternoon light, changing as he drove through shadows. He laughed, told me that he didn't remember. And I asked him then, if he wasn't afraid, just having to say that out loud.

I said, "My boyfriend does what he wants, I don't ask him. It's better that way."

He looked in the mirror and he asked me, "Oh yeah?"

And I told him, "Yes."

*She knew how he must be looking at her now. She could hear it in his voice and see it in the glance of his eyes. But when he spoke, she couldn't tell what words he said, through the taxi intercom. And when she spoke herself, her hands were sweating. She could have wiped them on the vinyl seats and seen her palm prints there. They might have faded slowly after she got out. There might have been a trace left by the time that someone else opened the door.∗

I looked at him then. I said, "If someone asked you to do a mad thing now, could you do it? Would you do it?"

His eyes were half caught with all the traffic, the lights, and with trying to look at me. There wasn't any trace of going home in them now. No trace of silence with his wife. And on every side of us, the people walked without looking. No one looks in London, but everyone sees. London is the pornographer. It gives you the fantasy, holds steady all the things that you need to believe in, long enough for you to take what you want.

"Would you do it?" I said.

"I don't know. Depends what, doesn't it? Depends –"

"If it was something that you'd remember for the rest of your life? Something that you might never have the chance to do ever again? Would you do it?" I said. "Now?"

He looked away from my reflection, out at London and every person moving there. He looked back at me. And then he said, "What?"

I've used pornography, used it with people, used it on my own. I like it put that way, in the same way that London will never be home, but you can use it to shape your life. I like the films though, not the magazines. A page doesn't cast light and shadow in your room, there's nothing to believe in on a page. Pornography shows you people, just the way that London shows you them. I like to think, when I watch it, that the people on the screen are watching me back. They could be the audience, as much as I am. And London, fantasy, pornographer, must be the audience as well. You could vomit on the street in London, and people would run their eyes over you, just like fingers. London is the audience, because it breathes and wets its mouth with fantasy, and every fantasy needs an audience to live.

I asked him, "How long is it since you had sex with someone apart from your wife?"

And while he laughed and sputtered, we were stopped at the traffic lights, caught between other black cabs, caught between other people's glances. Maybe they saw us.

His hands shifted on the wheel.

"I mean it," I said.

"What do you mean? You mean what?"

In front of us, the traffic lights changed. Traffic needs to move, we jolted forward.

I could see his shoulders and his tense neck, the way his hair shifted against his collar every time he shook his head. And I didn't care what his body would look like, and I couldn't really remember his face. I told you, we fucked that day, the city and I.

I said, "How long?" I said, "You could do something now, and you'd never forget it."

What is it about the things that aren't handed to you, that you want them so much more? And he was still laughing, still shaking his head, but there was something new in his movements now. I watched him. The things that aren't handed to you keep you running.

Maybe people, like engines, just need to be moving, and in London, no one stops. It's built to show you the things you want, the things that keep you moving. Try watching a porn movie, there's always someone who's just about to come.

Let me tell you how we parked up on Air Street, how he looked both ways, every way, before he got into the back of his cab. He wiped his hands on his trousers once he'd closed the door. He looked at me like he was scared, but I could have told him, you could have told him, there was nothing to be scared about. It's only fantasy, only porn.

Let me tell you, I want you to hear.

∗She saw spots of rain on the windows then. It would be raining on the little path that led to her front door. She thought, watching him shift as he tried to find answers to give her, of that little path, that door. When she looked out from there, the only view showed houses. There seemed to be a million of them, a million little paths. And she thought sometimes that, if London was the flickering screen, then all these houses she saw, they must be the silhouettes, the shadow shapes of a room, waiting to be seen in daylight again.∗

I said, "Pull over. Get in here."

"I'm not going to pull over, fuck's sake. You want to go home or not?"

"I told you what I want. Pull over, and get in here. And when you go home tonight, you won't be looking back at another day at work –" I wanted to tell him, it was only a fantasy, and how often do you get that chance? The chance to live one, to actually be one. I wanted to try and explain, this place was full of fantasy, and it was only right to live it, when you had that chance. It was right to try and be a part of it.

∗She kept thinking: London fucks you. London fucks everyone, every chance it gets. She kept thinking: Either you take it, or you take part.∗

The floor of a black cab is hard rubber, relief patterns, and I looked at it then. I drew my legs up. That floor would put marks on my knees, patterns in just the same shapes. And if there hadn't been glass between us, I would have reached out then, ran my own finger over his hairs. Tiny, soft little things on the back of his neck. I would have dug my fingernails into his skin. There was glass, though. And when I put my hand up and touched it, it was cold as a television screen.

∗She had touched the television screen once, she had put the flat of her hand against it and felt no flesh, no breath. The screen had been dry. Static electricity had flicked at her like a parody of movement.∗

He looked at my hand, pressed there. He could see it in the rearview mirror. And he was driving still, flicking glances from the road, to me. From London, to me. My hand must have been only three inches from those soft little hairs. Maybe the glass didn't even matter. He was tense now. Under his clothes, his shoulders were hardening up. On either side of us, London moved in grey rainwater, with grey, hunched bodies. The pavements, the roads, they felt like they could have squirmed with it. Air Street was there, up ahead.

"Pull in," I said. I didn't move my hand from the glass.

"Look, you don't understand. Fuck's sake, I can't –"

"You see it? There. Pull in there." I put my other hand up, framing his head with my fingers, on the other side of this glass. I swallowed. "I want to go home, see my boyfriend, and know that nothing about today was ordinary. I want to think about this, remember it. I want to do it, and go home and write every detail down. I want to write down, that you got in the back here, that you looked at me, reached out, touched me. I'll write, that you put your tongue in my mouth. That you put your fingers in my mouth. Pull over. There."

When he looked around us then, all he saw was London. There was nothing to stop him in what he saw. There was nothing out there that could break apart the things that I'd just said. What was out there, it made true the things that I'd said. It made them real.

And when he turned the wheel, his movements jerked, quick enough that he couldn't change his mind. I saw the side of his face for a moment as he pulled the cab in, but I didn't look at it long.

From Regent Street's bright, reflected sky, we came to stop. The arch of Air Street, damp, dark stone and broken pavements. And when he turned the engine off, I could hear the sound of people walking there. I could hear their voices in the traffic's noise, and they were shopping, walking, moving. London shows you the next thing, and the next, they couldn't stop. Think of a porn movie, five people fucking on screen. None of them can stop. You build a fantasy so fast, so constantly, that no one can step out. Are you ready to hear it? I'll show it to you, I'll tell you how it was.

I watched him turn the engine off, and he didn't sit for even a second. In front of the windscreen, Air Street closed us in. Dripping stone and scaffolding, buildings pressed almost close enough to touch. If their walls were faces, bodies, they would have been close enough to catch each other's breath.

I watched him get out and come around to my door. I ran a hand across my mouth and it was wet and my tongue wanted to move. My whole body wanted to move. They were built to move.

I opened the door for him, his face down, not looking at me. And that was when he ran his hands on his trouser legs. He stooped inside. He closed the door behind him. He sat on the seat next to me, and

she saw his dark eyes were lined with long lashes. The sort a wife might know well, might touch so gently as he slept, watch them flutter and be still, as he rested again.

I slid up to him. I put my hand around the back of his neck, the place that I'd seen, that I hadn't been able to touch for the glass. His skin was warm there, those soft little hairs tickled. And I did dig my fingernails in.

Outside, around us, there was rain. There was

noise. Everything in this place strains like a muscle strains, reaching for something that can't be touched. I dug my nails in, I moved across to him and I could hear his breathing. Quick, like he might jolt forward. Like engines, restrained.

I put his face up next to his face, and then I could feel his breathing. Another tiny inch, and his skin would be up against mine, his mouth would be up against mine. But I didn't move. I looked into his eyes, so close that there were no contours to his face. I held him there. I held myself there. His mouth was wet as mine. I saw it on his open lips.

I said, "Put your tongue out, the tip of your tongue, let me see."

His lip was shaking, oh so slight. And when he did it, I felt my own tongue move, like something in a mirror. Like we could echo each other, and still nothing but breath could pass between us. I would be the audience for him, I would watch every small movement his mouth made, and he would do the same for me, and still nothing would pass between us.

She had come, as some woman on the screen came, some woman with blonde hair. And her own fingers had moved too fast and too hard. They must have both felt the same thing then. The same straining, wanting thing.

So slowly, so perfectly slowly, I moved my mouth closer to his. Even his breathing was wet then. I put my hand on his leg.

"Ok," I said. "Ok ok. Touch my mouth with your

tongue. Gently, touch my lips, ok."

He tilted his head to do it. And when he put his face against mine, I could feel the stubble there. And when he put his tongue against mine, I could taste him, like static.

He moved his body closer, strained it closer. Twisted towards each other in the cab's back seat, his chest pressed on mine and I could feel the rub of skin underneath his clothes.

I pulled my hand from the back of his neck, scraped his skin as my fingers fell away, and then his hands were in my hair. Grabbing at it, like he could hold me still if he could only get enough of it in his hands. And my hands – my hands were under his shirt then. My fingers were on the hairs there, on the sides of his rib cage, breathing, breathing. The kind of rising, falling breath that makes you want to claw, grab, dig in hard enough that

there's no distance anymore

you're eating each other, mouths and skin and hands, eating away at each other, like you can't ever bite enough out. His tongue was in my mouth then, right the way in, all of it and I could feel his teeth and the softness of his lips, and all of it wet. Sharp or soft, all of it wet. All of it wanting.

I moved my fingers up his leg, other hand scraping fingernails on him. And he was trying to get closer. Pulling my hair. Kissing everything, mouth and cheek, uncaring, unaware. I moved my fingers up his leg, and through the cloth of his trousers, I felt it.

He arched.

Through the wetness on both of our faces, I pulled back. Just enough to speak, just enough for him to hear me through our breathing. You want to fuck me? You want to fuck now? Do you?

do you want me?

You want to fuck me now? Baby? I can feel you, you want to now. I can feel it. Baby.

And outside this metal and glass, every place around us, London strained. It reached. It wanted. It scraped with the noise of the cars and the buses, it was wet with the rain, with our kissing mouths. Outside Air Street's archway, there were people pressed so close. Close to each other, feeling it, not allowed to show the feeling. And close to us, to the shadows and reflections across the back window, so close to the place where we moved.

Fuck me now, yes, you want to. I know you want to, it's alright, you can do it. I want you to. It's alright, baby. It's alright to want it, I know you do. I can feel you wanting.

London fucks, all day and all night. It bucks with the movement of a million people. It fucks them, every single one of them, every moment that their eyes are open, it puts its fingers into them, its many tongues, and fucks them while they can't move or show that they feel it. While they can't even let their breathing change. And every grey, impassive face can feel it. It's in the flickers of doubt. It's in the way that they want to meet your eyes and have to turn away. London fucks every person here, while it holds their faces to the street.

I pressed my fingers there, into his crotch and moving oh so slightly, under his balls, cloth itching him. Around his dick.

That's it, baby. That's it. It's alright.

He strained. In his chest and his legs, in his mouth. And then I moved my fingers to his trouser fly. And he stopped straining. He stopped breathing. For a moment, I could feel him wanting nothing but

me

my hands.

I undid the button. Slow. So slow. I stopped. I reached up under the line of my skirt, as he sat, immobile, watching only. In front of his eyes and his open lips, I pulled my underwear away. I dropped it on the cab floor, in shadow there. And then I moved to sit on top of him. Both fingers in his fly, unzipping, both hands inside, and my mouth all over his mouth again. His fingers in my hair, needing me.

That's it. That's right.

Do you want to hear it now? I'll tell you how it felt.

She couldn't get his dick inside her, sitting up on him like that. She had to pull him down onto the floor, where dirty shoes had left smears of cold water, her own shoes, and other people's.

I went down on all fours, with his hands still in my hair that way, and I felt him pull his trousers down, felt the prickle of the hair on his thighs. He put his fingers on my hip, trying to find skin, trying to find something he could grip and hold onto. And when he'd found his grip, he could push himself in. And he did. Kneeling, I felt him. In a little. In a little more, and then he was fucking me. A little more. Again.

∗She had to let him do it from behind, too dry to be fucked in any way but the easiest. With her head down, she saw the ridged patterns on the floor of the cab. She let him fuck her, too dry to feel anything but pain. Somewhere underneath those patterns, the paving stones let filthy water trickle, out under this arch, and into Regent Street, under other people's feet. Like tearing, that was how it felt as she let him do it. She thought about the woman on screen, the woman with the blonde hair. They have drugs, for making porn movies, pills that send the blood down into the crotch and give a penis an erection, fills the walls of a vagina with enough blood to make it swell. She didn't look like that on screen, like she might have taken drugs. On screen, everything was very brightly lit. Watching it, she hadn't been able to see the line where the set ended. There was a line, though. The carpet in shot was taped down to a hard floor, scuffed around the edges by the shuffling feet of soundmen and cameramen and the boy that brought the coffee in. London shines with dirt and chrome, like every part of it is lit with stage lights. But there is a line where London stops, and only houses carry on. A million rows of houses, like an audience, gathered to watch, hands up against a glass screen. She lived in that kind of row. The kind where grass and weeds struggle around the path and there are four locks on every door.

Her front door was painted blue, it was heavy, made of metal. There were skips parked outside, rainwater running now down their sides. Grey sky showed in the windows where she lived. It reflected there, with no lights on in the rooms inside. Behind her front door, the carpet was dim, mail strewn in piles. Behind her front door, there was silence. It settled like cold, in rooms where no one else had ever talked or fucked or slept.

In the kitchen, there was a photograph, stuck to the fridge. It showed the place where she'd grown up.∗

I felt him, moving faster. On my hips, his fingers gripped and loosened, every time he moved. And the sound of his breathing was little groans now. Little moans, and I was telling him, yes, you move, you moan, it feels good, doesn't it feel good? Little needful groans that got faster. And he fucked harder, and he was saying things, saying words then, saying yes. I want it. Let me come. I want to come. He was swearing over and over then. Fuck. Yes. Yes. He was coming, and he told me. I'm coming. Now. Please.

Fuck.

Outside, they must have seen us. They must have heard us and felt us. And knowing, they must have walked past, trying not to let it show on their faces that they could feel themselves, all the more clearly for his dick in me.

He shivered when he came. He purred. He let it go.

That was how it felt. Can you feel it? I want you

to feel it, I want you to know. How many chances are there to be part of a fantasy? I was part of a fantasy that day. Every fantasy must have an audience, it must have one, just to live. To be real. This one was mine. Tell me, please. How do you feel?

Rebecca Ray is author of *A Certain Age*.

a soft-cotton yarn

James Flint

This season, detail counts – feathers, frills and contrast linings are the perfect foil to sleek black tailoring.[1]

He is sitting in the reception area of the branch of White Cross Dentists that's opposite the Angel tube watching a Britney video on VH-1. There are four black Goldstar® television monitors which it's possible to watch Britney on. They are large and black and look like flying bugs. Two of them hang from ceiling brackets secured above the Enquiries Desk (which our hero eyes lazily and suspects is manufactured out of moulded pinewood, though it may be silver elm). A third hangs in the north-western corner of the room right above his head: he can't watch that one but he can feel its furry electromagnetic presence and sense its neck-snapping potential energy like it's some televisual Sword of Damocles[2] or something. The fourth and final set (though not by any means the final TV in the building – our hero knows from experience that similar glass and steel black cubes of visual delight hang above each and

[1]   All stand-alone italics are taken from the *Littlewoods Autumn & Winter 2000* catalogue.
[2]   A classical idiom generally used to mean an impending disaster. The sword itself was the sword beneath which the sycophant Damocles was said to have been forced to sit by the Syracusian tyrant Dionysis, in order that he the king might demonstrate that to be a king was not the happy and carefree state Damocles had claimed it was. This important lesson was driven home by having the sword in question suspended vertically by means of single human hair tied at one end to its pommel and at the other to a fixture in a roofbeam (I imagine). The chair in which Damocles was forced to sit, needless to say, was positioned in such a way that the weapon's sharp tip hovered directly above the crown of the sycophant's unprotected head.

every one of the dove grey dentist's chairs that swivel and recline in the dozen or so treatment rooms that are to be found beyond the dove grey door marked *Surgeries*[3])[4] is located directly to the east, the knowledge of which bearing our hero would quickly be apprised were he to take out from his pocket the small compass he carries on his key ring (a compass won from a Christmas cracker, Christmas 1998, and not often used, though its constituent elements [magnetised needle and disc of printed card marked with the four cardinal points and their appropriate subdivisions, no need to list them here] are properly oriented with regard to one another and do actually function).[5] The other people in here with him number nine [or on occasion ten].

Two [three] of these bodies are to be found, at the particular instant we're describing, behind the moulded pinewood/silver elm Enquiries Desk. One of them [the one in the square brackets] is in the process of moving between the area behind the counter already occupied by two seated colleagues and a second room (the adjacent office) which our hero (who does have a

3   Which door will feature in the story a little later on.
4   Which televisions are to a large degree responsible for ensuring our hero's continued patronage of this particular dental establishment.
5   Though they probably would not function, not here and now, because of the disruptive field effects created by the four bug-like televisions hanging from the ceiling of the reception room and the three telephones and two computers located behind the Enquiries Desk and the fax machine and photocopier in the office adjacent to it and the underground railway

name but which name is not important) assumes from the way this woman sort of sidles in and out of it is in fact quite small and perhaps cluttered with shelves and filing systems and/or more electronic equipment. This woman moving out to in has the flat blue cheeks, the oval spectacles, the hastily knotted graying ponytail and the slightly boss eyes of a person who's in charge. What she says goes, our hero realises, as he watches her peer authoritatively over the shoulders of the two receptionists (who are dressed in white, like nurses, to help lend the reception area the appropriate air of medical efficiency). These two receptionists are younger and prettier than their superior. Their uniforms are uniforms: one-piece dresses with short-sleeved arms and zips up the back. The superior, on the other hand, wears a doctor's coat and wears it open, revealing her own civvies underneath. 'I'm responsible and in control,' this outfit says. 'I understand this operation enough to know when it is required of me for cultural and/or hygienic reasons to keep my coat buttoned and when it is acceptable to leave it open to help relieve some of the enormous stress I experience on a daily

line that runs beneath the building not to mention the electric current carried by the wiring in the walls and floor and ceiling plus all the stuff outside in the street including the cabling for the streetlamps and all the various telecoms along with the gas mains and water mains and then on top of that the cars and trucks and buses driving past which also have an electromagnetic signature as do the cellphones in the pockets of the other people in the reception room itself (our hero being one of these) as do the surrounding cellphone base stations and television and radio transmitters and so on.

basis due to the enormous workload and weighty responsibilities placed upon my shoulders.' It also suggests that the receptionists are not intelligent and/or experienced enough to understand the boundaries and protocols of this coat-closed/coat-open thing. Hence their all-in-ones, which relieve them of the need to understand this and so prevent mistakes from being made – which speaks again in favour of the establishment's professionalism and efficiency. 'We know what we're doing here,' these clothes all say. 'We are capable. You can trust us with those most fragile and personal parts of you. Your teeth.' One of the receptionists is black and one is white, our hero also notes. This lends the Enquiries Desk a pleasing inter-cultural harmony and balance.

Leather is big news this season – we've got the latest catwalk looks all at super value prices.

Britney bounces across the three [four] screens, more real to our hero than any of the other people in here. These other people are:
• The two [three] women sitting [standing] behind the moulded pinewood (silver elm?) Enquiries Desk.
• A bright executive-type woman with cropped and bleached white hair, who wears a tailored navy wool-blend business suit and patent leather court shoes. She's concentrating on whatever it is that's displayed on the LCD screen of her cherry-transparent Handspring® PDA. Her face is the colour and shape of

a lone butternut squash, although her nose is something of an anomaly: its skin seems draped over a skeleton of coat-hanger wire. She is nervous and on edge.

• A mother and son. Mother = young mum, dressed as if for going clubbing. She wears a black padded gilet with zip fastening, two side pockets and a drawcord hem (undrawn) over an Everlast™ long-sleeved V-neck top with logo to arm and a utility skirt with drawcord to waist and hem (drawn), front pocket and zip front detail. (100% Nylon). (Steel grey). The boy (six) slumps/lies in the curve of his purple Ikea chair dangling his feet and staring with unmasked contempt at the executive-type woman opposite. His head is drawn back like a turtle's into the carapace of his voluminous Scott and Fox padded jacket with nylon shell and duck down and feather filling. A fleece hat is stretched tight across his skull. This hat is dark blue and embroidered with the words 'Street Racer' in a different colour (white). The boy is imitating the sound of a car by forcing a stream of air through pursed lips and his mother is not telling him to stop doing this.

• A young man here for a root canal. He has never had a root canal before, nor any kind of major dental operation. He is apprehensive and even slightly frightened. He has pale hair, a crabbed posture, lightly freckled skin and an Ericsson T18 cellphone in his pocket. He is frail to look at, but it is not the promise of pain that frightens him for he understands the power of Xylocaine©.[6] What frightens him is the worry of making somehow the *wrong decision* about the kind of cap to get once his delinquent tooth has been operated on and the nerve removed. Should he go for classic gold, which is not only the safest option and the cheapest and probably from a pure comfort point of view the best but which would add a hint of pimp-*chic* to his smile? Would that be good? Would that make him more attractive? Or would it make him look run-down, a little seedy? It might go down quite well in England but what if he emigrated to America? What then? Orthodontic perfection is valued extremely highly in the United States. He has no immediate plans to emigrate but you never know. Oral perfection would demand he opt for porcelain. But he's read somewhere that it's whitened with uranium, the porcelain, meaning he'd be allowing a beta radiation source to be permanently inserted into his mouth. Which seems a heavy price to pay for looking pure and natural and conforming with mainstream North American aesthetico-dental standards. It's a conundrum, certainly, and he was hoping not to have to ponder it, he was hoping just to turn up and have the dentist decide for him one way or the other. But the dentists are all running late today because the weekend's torrential rainfall has resulted in

6   Tradename for lignocaine.

London's Underground becoming badly flooded. The capital's in chaos, an atmosphere of crisis pervades the land. The people here are mostly local people. The dentists mostly commute.

• An older man, decrepit, skin like hessian, dressed in Oxfam. His cheeks work at the air like tired bellows, his body is a teetering shack of sinew and worn bones. He doesn't have an appointment, he's just sort of wandered in from off the street seeking refuge from the rain. He doesn't know it but he's got about three minutes thirty before the boss-woman behind the desk comes over and kicks him back out into the weather. He's been watching the young boy opposite through cloudy eyes, his gnarly brow intent with jealousy. He wants to make that car noise too. He used to be able to make that noise, he remembers. But he can't seem to get the muscles in his lips to tighten up enough, not these days. Not any more. On the wall above his head is a glass light fixture in Klein blue.

• An Asian gentleman who is slowly being driven insane by the sound of the six-year-old's car imitation, which he interprets not as being an attempt to mimic a car's engine noise at all but as impression of the sound of a dentist's drill. (His own fears and preoccupations are perhaps speaking to him here.) This boy, he reasons, is deliberately trying to wind us (me) up. He's too young to know the trauma of the dentist's drill. He's too young to realise. In my family such behaviour would not be tolerated. Why doesn't his mother shut him up?

• A gigantic woman hovering beneath a fringed cap of

113

lacquered curls. Her very bulk is a denial of gravity; she doesn't so much sit as bob a few inches above the ground. Her skin is oily but clear of pimples, her skirt did service once, perhaps, as a parachute. When our hero looks at her breasts he thinks: Zeppelin. When the young man with the freckles and crabbed posture breaks from his cap conundrum to imagine the possibility of sexual relations with this woman he becomes more frightened still. The woman is not worried by the poverty of either man's imagination. She's preoccupied with the smell emanating from the decrepit streetperson sitting just two seats away from her beneath the glass lighting fixture in Klein blue. He smells of urine, naphthalene, stale tobacco, rotten fruit and methylated spirits. And those are just the odours she can identify. He smells unhealthy, that's what it is. Unhealthy. Unacceptable, in here. Shouldn't someone really do something about it? Someone really?

Pale, interesting and very now – the biker goes glam.

Beneath our hero's chair our hero's placed his motorcycle helmet. Outside in the street in a motorcycle bay (in the street a few streets away) he's parked his motorcycle. It is a 1993 purple Honda CruiseKing with purple plastic cowling that is faded but not cracked (our hero has never crashed) and a built in radio-cassette (pretty upmarket at the time). Two water-resistant loudspeakers are built into the black plastic fascia. There's a purple fuel tank, a long black leather seat with passenger lumbar support and a non-integrated purple back-box and two non-integrated purple panniers one of which (the left-hand, as you're driving), is at this moment sitting in the hall cupboard in our hero's home, on account of how it has a broken fastener-clasp-lock-catch type thing[7] and won't stay closed. Our hero's favourite thing about this bike is not the wheels of carbon reinforced epoxy[8] with aluminium hubs nor the idling throb the frame transmits to his thighs[9] and lower body at traffic lights,[10] nor the spangly stars and stripes 'V for victory' hand signal sticker he's affixed to the purple fibreglass of the back-box, but: the radio-cassette because of the way it enables him, as he drives around listening to his favourite shows on Capital and Heart,[11] to make this little focal point of sound so that people turn their heads.

Friends have told him that when he's got his

---

[7]   Damaged when someone broke into the pannier and stole the winter weight thermal biker mitts, Dremel corded multi-tool with 40 interchangeable heads and two CDs (R.E.M.;Gomez) stored therein.

[8]   This material has a very high flexural strength, better than that of steel.

[9]   He's sort of short and slightly plump, our hero, and his thighs tend to chafe a little when he walks (a legacy of an enthusiastic period of gym abuse in his early twenties followed up by a draining 9-5 and too many Menu Master meals). He's a cheery sort, and likes to smile, and has wide blue eyes which are bright as they look about the place. The light has this way of reflecting off their lacquer-like glaze.

[10]   Though this sensation does, he must admit, jostle for that coveted position of most favoured aspect/thing.

[11]   95.8 FM and 106.2 FM respectively.

115

helmet on he looks like William Hague.[12]

Friends have told him that with his helmet off he looks even more like William Hague.

While he's been waiting for the dentists to arrive, the dentists delayed by rain, our hero's been leafing through various magazines and trying to remember all the words to 'Coward of the County'. He's just here for a check-up, he's not in any kind of pain, and he doesn't mind the waiting either because he's in no hurry to get to work. (He has this job, it's not important what it is, but it is not dissimilar in nature to the job you do). He's flicked his way through *Elle Decoration* and *Woman* and *Red* and *Hello* and *Marie-Claire* and he's given up on 'Coward of the County' and is trying to recall instead the full lyrics to Don McLean's 'American Pie', comparatively a much easier challenge because of how Madonna's just put a cover version out which our hero's heard played on the radio (on his motorcycle's radio-cassette) six perhaps seven times in the last day or two. Strangely though, while some considerable time has passed since he's been sitting here in this waiting room, whenever he looks up at VH-1 (which has been playing with the sound turned off) it's always Britney dancing up there, still. A Britney special, possibly? He doesn't know. He couldn't tell.

---

[12] Especially now he's had his thin blond hair, for a long time now looped by male pattern baldness into an edge ecology of grassy dunes and damp sandy hollows, cut really short.

Find your size by being measured around the palm. The measurement in inches will be your size.

The magazines haven't grabbed him, really, apart for the interiors in *Elle Decoration* for a while and an article about how housework is the new sex in *Red*, a notion with which our hero can identify, being something of a maven for general tidiness himself. But what has really caught his fancy[13] is the *Littlewoods Autumn & Winter 2000* catalogue, which somebody must have left in there, seeing as how I can't imagine White Cross Dentists would have ordered it unless it was forced upon them[14] by a typically stubborn and cyclically recalescent Littlewoods marketing campaign, which now that I think about it is actually quite likely. One of the staff might I suppose have bought it in from home. It really doesn't matter much. Forget about it, I would if I were you. I already have.

Great Value! *Packs of eight cotton-rich socks in two sizes and three colourways. £9.*

So our hero's sitting there, locked into his catalogue, and outside the rain is still coming down, and he's just discovered that sandwiched between the *Men's Shoes*

[13]   and which even he'll admit's no big surprise.
[14]   I'm sorry but I still can't get used to referring to companies as 'it'.

section that he first opened to and *Men's Nightwear* is a small (two page) section dedicated to motorcycle clothing. Which just happens to feature, he's surprised to see, the very OGK helmet featuring unique aeroblade airflow spoiler and diffuser[15] system, alloy-tech composite outershell, bespoke cheek pad fitting, quick release Ejector Visor®, Double-D retention and brow and chin ventilation[16] he's long been coveting. Although the one pictured is in the Red-multi colour scheme and the one he actually desires is basic black: he thinks (and rightly) that the Red-multi OGK's kind of a poser's lid. Still, the price is pretty good and, he notes, if he orders from the catalogue he has the added options of paying over 20, 34 or 100 weeks (29.9% APR).

There's also as well on the facing page a rather fine pair of Akito 'Cougar' pants and matching jacket, which are (it says) Airdura® 100% breathable garments which sounds pretty cool just by itself even if you don't factor in the CE Bodyguard® body armour for shoulders, elbows, kidneys (*kidneys!*) and knees, the zipout thermal liner (in the jacket, which jacket will zip together with the pants to form a combo suit), the multi waterproof pockets (again in the jacket, and our hero is confused here because does that mean multi pockets or pockets that are waterproof for multi types of rain?) and

---

[15]   Closeable.
[16]   Also closeable.

the rear back pouch (again that's jacket).

Our hero looks at the model who is wearing this and thinks he's looking pretty cool.

And then notes he's carrying a red-multi OGK AASD. Which fact throws our hero for a moment, until he realises this bloke must by definition be something of a poser, since he's a model, which is a poser occupation, so yes, he does look like a poser (since he is one), this bloke, and is perhaps not someone our hero thinks he should try to emulate. Which means he stays with basic black as his helmet colour scheme of choice, though he still thinks the Cougar suit is completely where it's at, especially when he looks down at his own rain-saturated leather motorcycle jeans across which the *Littlewoods* catalogue is lying slumped[17] and on account of the moisture seeping from them is also (though our hero doesn't know it yet) somewhat stuck to. These leather motorcycle jeans which he's had for some five years now.

And which long ago started to bag out un-controllably at the knee, he now accepts.

At which juncture it strikes our hero that he can't remember ever seeing a pair of leather trousers, his own or anybody else's, that *didn't* bag out at the knee. That bagging out at the knee seems in fact to be

---

[17] This slumping effect due to catalogue's being made up of one thousand twelve hundred and fifty-nine glue-bound pages printed with four-colour process Accolade® lightweight coated paper.

just a necessary truth about leather trousers, an *a priori*
tendency, even with the Mercury Mega leathers featured
right here in the catalogue which must be absolutely
brand new and are maybe even tailored to the bloke
that's wearing them (which bloke reminds our hero of
this kid he used to know at school and who he always
hated and who couldn't be mistaken for anything but an
errant poser not like the other bloke in the Cougar stuff
who even though he's carrying an OGK AASD helmet in
Red-multi instead of basic black could still be
construed as cool) but which are already bagging out.
All of which makes our hero wonder if perhaps leather's
time has come.

*Soft-cotton yarn with built-in stretch for extra comfort
and a brilliant fit.*

Inevitably, as if tugged by an invisible force from the
vortex of pleasure he's created[18] by having mentally
placed himself in the position of the model sporting the
Cougar combo and imagining how that particular cut of

---

[18]   A vortex with low torque, admittedly
[19]   It should be mentioned here that the pleasure
quotient was upped a fair bit when our hero spied the pair of
Belstaff 'Viper' booties with side Velcro®-fastening and
Aero-tex® lining plus a gear change toe reinforcement and oil-
resistant soles and in his imagination slipped those on his feet,
exchanging them for that pair of old and trusty but
fundamentally pretty fucked now low-cut Dockers®. Pleasure
vortex rotational speed was increased a further notch when he
substituted a Grex 'Coast Highway Patrol'[19a] helmet (£199.00 or
£9.95 over 20 weeks, £5.24 over 38 wks etc etc.) in black and
wineberry with US-style open face inc. Lexan shell and flying

Airdura® fabric (w/ thermal lining, bodyarmour, multi-pockets and back pouch etc.) might actually feel,[19] our hero finds himself slowly leafing backwards through the catalogue, back through *Men's Nightwear* with its flat lit photographs of Lycra® trunks and vented boxers and stretch piqué packs of three, back through shirts and suits,[20] back through *Casual*, *Jeanswear* and *Definitions*® and back through *Kids* at which point he gives up on trying to resist and inserting his finger about a centimetre from the catalogue's front cover flips a wad of Accolade® lightweight coated pages across his lap from left over to right and lands right-side up (still mentally clothed in the Akito 'Cougar' combo [zipped together in jumpsuit mode], Viper boots and that Grex CHP black and wineberry open-face) in *Style Unlimited (ladies)*.

A wonderfully wearable viscose shirt in a striking graphic print. Why not team it with our luxurious soft-touch cupro separates?

eagle sticker on the crown for that red-multi OGK AASD number which he still couldn't really see himself coming round to, even despite the what was really a remarkably good price, considering, though it would depend of course on what they charged for delivery.

19a   Which moniker presumably came about in an attempt to allude to the popular 1980s US TV-show CHiPs where the CHP stands for 'California Highway Patrol' without being able to use that phrase exactly for copyright infringement and/or trade description reasons.

20   This section actually subdivided into 'Principles' and 'Classics'.

Having given in to temptation, finally, our hero has gained the freedom to explore. Carefully he patrols the delightful glades of Machine Wash Easy Care and Dry Clean Only. Gingerly he picks his way through mix-and-match, stretch flannel in grey marl, easy-wear bi-stretch fabrics and wardrobe essentials all in two colours. Musing to himself the soft musings of a late-thirty-something single man he wanders the avenues of *Berkertex®* and 'Luxury Touch' cupro fabrics and finds himself wishing, perhaps strangely, that his own body might too know the feel of these items of at once exotic and familiar clothing. What exactly is it like, he wonders, the sensation of having one's feet embraced by court shoes with stretch vamp in black or navy, heel height 2 1/2 in. approx.? Or of having one's nipples gently chafed by that colour-block long sleeved tunic blouse in sheer viscose georgette? But sadly these aspects of reality are well out of his reach. These are truths, experiences, which will be always beyond him.

Wool rich with Lycra®.

Who are these women? He flips through the groves of pretty-rather-than-beautiful females with their Woolmark endorsements and their five subjective modes. These modes are:

1. *Demure*; gaze directed just below the camera lens.
2. *Submissive*; gaze directed either at the floor or (more chargedly) at groin of the viewer/photographer.

3. *Careworn-but-Happy*; gaze directed out of shot (shot left, usually) at (it is to be imagined) the husband/long-term boyfriend/children.
4. *Apprehensive*; gaze directed out of shot (shot right) where is occurring something that is morally questionable and yet unquestionably titillating, the attempt to solve the libidinal conundrum thus presented being clearly present in the eyes.
5. *Mild-Defiant*; gaze directed straight back at viewer/photographer in a brave show of spirit that cannot yet disguise the fear that such deliberate eye-to-eye contact invites retaliation, even violence, violation.

It seems they're wearing an invisible purdah of some sort, all these women. They seem to our hero to have been educated to mould themselves to his most stubborn and impacted patriarchal desires.

The brand with attitude, fun, sexy, fashion, feel special in luxurious lace.

The underwear sections, when our hero gets to them, are too intense even for him. The women here only do Demure or Mild-Defiant. But the modes differ in crucial ways from their counterparts in Outerwear: there's a playful wetness about Demure that's present here, a willingness that stops it shading into Submissive and at the same time communicates (and this, our hero thinks, is where these models earn their money; this is a look that can't be easy to achieve) at the same time communicates a subtle but unmistakable sense of despite-me-being-in-your-power-there's-a-good-chance-that-sex-won't-happen kind of feeling.

This suggestion of ultimate frustration is a massive turn-on, our hero finds.

With Mild-Defiant, on the other hand, the understanding that I-know-you're-going-to-take-me-violently so central to the women's expressions previously has vanished with the clothes.[21] Snugly cupped by white or flame full cup underwired bras and deep briefs from the Gypsy range or cream bodyshapers in Meryl® microfibre with suspenders and detachable straps, the shadows of their aureolae just visible through mesh veils of 73% polyamide, 24% polyester and 3% elastane luxurious lace finished in a tattoo effect,[22] the eyes tell a different story. Now that the clothes are off, they firmly inform you, we are no longer playing. I am a woman and you are a man, from here on out there will be a desperation and seriousness in our love making that is proper to fine and fit and strong young animals such as you and I. You'll need to be sure you can satisfy me before you dare to slip your hand up beneath my unpadded bandeau…

Two things make our hero turn from the

---

[21]   In the light of these fresh observations it would be perhaps more sensible to divide Demure into two subcategories: Demure[Outerwear] and Demure[Underwear] (and, correspondingly, to split Mild-Defiant into Mild-Defiant[o] and Mild-Defiant[u]).

[22]   the pubis a faded handprint on the crotch.

Underwear section back to *Jeanswear*. The first is a small black and white icon of a measuring tape underneath which are the words: 'Your bra size can alter so it's important to measure yourself correctly and regularly.' These words conjure in our hero an image of these women, naked, measuring themselves (and each other) so vivid in its detail that the catalogue is in danger of being dislodged from his lap.[23] The second is a photograph of his favourite woman so far, a caramel-skinned fox with translucent Braeburn apple-red cheeks, dark caterpillar brows, delicate, delectable Hubba-Bubba® pink lips and a kitten's profile, dressed in a Triumph International® 'Amourette' underwired brassiere in stretch tectronic lace with a peephole rose front and matching maxi briefs with continuous pansy-pattern, which picture is unbearably sexy not because of the woman in particular or even the *de-luxe* lingerie but because of that single word 'Amourette', a word which speaks to our hero of the succulent, forbidden centres of exclusive chocolate liqueurs that once released from their dark Belgian prisons quickly escape the portcullises of professionally whitened teeth and overwhelm the curtain walls of dewy high-gloss lips to run in candy rivulets across the furry down of dusty Tuscan chins where they're dammed by single perfect

23   Or would be if it wasn't stuck to it.

painted fingernails at the soft climax of slow dinners lit by candlelight which have unravelled on crepuscular balconies lost deep in Marbellan hills beneath soft Spanish moons that hover above ever tranquil seas while the aromatic scent of pine drifts in caressing, tangy fronds through the heavy, sultry air. Oh god.

Snake print and ruffles are fashion must-haves – this fabulous dress has the lot.

So he flips back to *Jeanswear*, our hero does, thinking it's maybe time to turn the volume down a little. But as luck would have it the page he turns to already has her featured there, dressed this time in a long-sleeved blouse with pop-buttons in Soviet-blue and a pair of stretch bootcut denims (stonewash). He turns the page and she's there again, modelling a white V-necked tee beneath a Blue Star® 'Western' jacket w/ front and side pocket detail, a wardrobe basic in ring spun denim, coloured twill or this season's marl fabric, great value at £25. Turning again he comes upon her pert buttocks, set off to wonderful advantage by a pair of indigo stretch capris with side-zip fastening and narrow waistband (washable), the trousers everybody wants.[24] On into *Camisoles* – in lemon, biscuit and dark-olive – and she's

---

[24] Now available cropped or full-length.

waiting, hand at her neck, sunlight in her hair. She leans against a white picket fence in Holiday Shop, wearing a Sweet lavender-print fit 'n' flare viscose dress with tie back for more flattering aspect, available in two colours/two lengths. A pair of silver and lilac daisy-thong sandals kiss her angelic little feet.

This is followed by three pictures in narrative sequence:

1. **Her leaning casually but guardedly against that white picket fence** [Colourway: Sweet lavender-print; Expression: Submissive – Floor];

2. **Her walking towards him over a shadow pattern of overhead tree branches dappled across the dust by a delicate summer light** [Colourway: Sweet lavender-print; Expression: Mild-Defiant – Clothed];

3. **Her walking away but looking back, showing the garment's bowed tie-back and revealing back slit** [Colourway: Lemon-print; Expression: a new mode, call it mode 6, 'Chase-Me'].

I want… This season's **must have** fashion item.

So it's a pursuit she wants, is it? If so, our hero will gladly oblige. Dental appointment forgotten he sets off after her, the sleeves of his Airdura® Akito 'Cougar' jacket making small *schwiping* sounds as he hurries in the wake of the gambolling lovely through several dozen glossy catalogue pages – *schwip schwip* – following the trail laid by her discarded garments: a cerise bikini top w/ halter neck tie fastening she's let fall in *Swimwear*, a pair of 58% PVC trousers still warm from her legs in *Morgan de Toi*, a fully lined bias cut crochet dress in steel mesh draped over the page divide in *Great Brands*, a pair of black-red-snakeskin inside-zip ankle boots with centre seam detail and new fashion heel, in *Rock Chick*. And all this while the sense that she's never more than two or three pages ahead does not desert him and all this while her Chloe Narcisse, a fragrance for women by Karl Lagerfield, seemingly enfolds his head. *Schwip schwip*.

Not until he finds an oil-slick backless cami in two tonal colours is he sure he's cornered her, that and a flocked dress with boob tube handkerchief upper body styling. Just one more page – *schwip* – just one – yes look, a lone glitter hanky top, easy to wear – schwip –– just one more page, just one… cautiously now, don't want to scare her, just one more page – *schwip* – just one…

But it's a trick! She's not here! The trail is a false one! Somehow she's mislead him, coaxed him all the way through *TopShop*® and steered him on into *Miss Teen*. He flips forwards hurriedly through the pages of teenagers, each one sexless and arid as a frozen Himalayan plateau. She's escaped! She has fooled him! He scrunches a bunch of easy-tear fashion plates in his hand. She has given him the slip!

For the first time for some while he looks up from the catalogue, his reinforced Viper boot tips toeing at the crumbling lip of a plummeting precipice of despair. He stares into space. His tooth starts to ache, as if to remind him that back in reality there are more serious matters to be attended to.

But then he sees her. She's there. She's there in the room with him, over there at the Enquiries Desk, standing slightly folded at the waist, listening to the receptionist who is giving her some piece of information. She rests one delicate hand on the moulded pinewood[25] of the counter. Her hair is tied back with a mauve velvet scrunchy. Britney is still dancing, in a school uniform, just over her head. She's wearing scarlet leather bar shoes with touch fastening detail and new lightweight wedge soles, silver grey flat front satin slacks, a cashmere-feel beaded knit[26] in Hot-pink multi and a reversible gilet in techno fabric and fake fur (polyester lining side out, Baby Seal-blue). She finishes speaking with the receptionist, straightens up, turns his way. She has come for him.

Body Sculpture® Elliptical Walker w/ adjustable tension for variable resistance. Dual-action arms give an upper body workout, can also be locked in a static position for improving lower body and hips. Low impact exerciser. Racing computer with three motivating programmes. Large non-slip footplates. £139.

25   though it may equally be silver elm.
26   'A luxury everyone can afford.'

She beckons him. He stands. She indicates that the catalogue is stuck to his leather trousers and tells him with a complex but unmisinterpretable wave of her hand that he should detach it and bring it to her. Like a prize. He bends, peels it off, leaves the back-cover advertisement for One2One Pay-As-You-Go Cellphones reverse-printed on the front of his right thigh. He holds the catalogue schoolboy-like in both hands. She communicates with her eyes that he should come to her. The other nine [ten] people in the White Cross Dentists' reception seem strangely frozen in time.

'Should I bring my helmet?' he asks, perhaps a little timidly, and glances back at the Grex CHP black and wineberry open-face sitting there abandoned on the floor.

'No,' she tells him (the first time he's heard her voice). 'Don't bring the helmet. Just come.'

He follows her, for real this time. She opens the dove grey door marked Surgeries and jogs through it: he arrives just before it completes its back-swing and goes through as well. He finds himself in a narrow corridor, three doors and a stairway leading off, a corridor familiar from the many times he's been here for his dental check-ups. He glimpses a triangle of silver grey satin and the thick end of a lightweight wedge sole disappearing around the far corner. He rounds that corner too, sees the same black and grey triangles disappearing into a room.

He arrives outside the room. There's a small brown plastic plaque that reads 'Dr. Reynolds' slotted into the small brown plastic plaque holder affixed to the door. There's a long thin window set into the door, a window the glass of which is reinforced with embedded wire so it looks like graph paper or the strings of a tennis racket. Our hero peers through the strings. Inside our heroine is waiting for him. She is slowly removing all of her clothes.

He draws a deep breath, and enters.

Extra-wide double oven cooker with timer and auto-switch 'safety off' when toughened lid is closed.

He imagines she'll want him to take her while she reclines in the dentist's chair. But this is not the case.

'No, no,' she tells him, as he gesticulates in its direction. 'Not there. Over here.' She slips past him on tiptoe, breasts cadencing like bubbles of softest silk, her hair wafting out as if blown by breezes emanating from the fair cheeks of cherubim. 'Here,' she says, bending over the consultancy table. 'And give me that.' Taking the catalogue from him she lays it open on the tan Formica®-topped surface. It falls open at *Victorian Lighting*. She grips the table's bevelled ash[27] edges with both hands, arches her back into an injection-moulded concavity, sets her feet perhaps twenty inches apart and

---

27   Or possibly moulded pinewood.

presents him with the twin bowls of her ivory rump.

Enraptured, he gazes down upon her fair form. The combo Hot-pink multi and dense black real curl-effect of her womanhood reminds him of a chine cut of lamb he'd seen earlier, roasting to crisp and delicious perfection inside a Parkinson Cowan single-cavity window oven with fan assist and easy-clean finish on page 924.

'Would you like me to take off my suit?' he asks, clumsily.

'Lounging Lady' in bronze-effect finish, lounging on a real Tiffany glass bed. Requires 2 x 25 watt candle bulbs. H 28 cms, W 33 cms approx.

'I like it on,' she tells him, 'and now shush while I read to you.' He shushes and with trembling fingers tries to undo his fly.

'"Victoriana" wall light with "snowflake" glass shades,' she begins as he struggles with the Velcro® all-weather protector flap. 'Glass-bead trim and antique-look brassed metalwork that matches items 2, 3 and 4. Maximum sixty watt bulb,' she adds as finally he locates the head of the zipper and wrestles it down.

While he frees his member from the unforgiving vents and layers of brand-new Airdura® 100% breathable material she speaks to him of multi-gyms and winter-weight mattresses, of four door sliding wardrobes with pine-effect panelled doors, of upholstery and floorcoverings, of Breville® waffle irons, of non-stick frying pans, of variable speed jigsaws with pendulum action, of slim profile vacuum cleaners light enough to store on a bracket affixed to the wall.

But now he's out of his confines and bobbing free in the antiseptic air. As he reaches for her hips and positions himself ready for entry the phosphorescent light from the dental X-ray viewing panel which someone's left on illuminates his stubby manhood with a pale medicinal glow. 'A topspeed food processor with a unique mixing action for perfect kneading, mixing, whisking and much more,' she gasps as he makes contact, her voice deepening mid-sentence into a throaty whisper. 'With, uh, with a – *uhmph* – 4.4 litre D-shaped kenlyte bowl – *ahhh, ahhhh* – and unique planetary mixing action. And... *ooogch*... three... *frrrcchhh*... additional... concealed... power... outlets... *mmnngg*.'

Top brand quality variable steam/spray/surge iron with easy-glide non-stick soleplate, anti-drip system and constant steam pressure for great performance even when you're low on water.

'Speak to me of cleaning appliances,' he begs her and so she does, telling him of the Smartvac 1484 with backsaver handle, 15-in fastrack[28] for faster cleaning, 3-

---

28   15-in FASTRACK cut cleaning time by 25% when compared with other cleaners.

stage HEPA micro filter and integrated stair cleaning hose. Avbl. in Moroccan Green/Colombian White. 'Sing to me of luggage,' he pants, and she tongues out descriptions of rubber backed 600-denier polyester trolley cases with push button mechanisms and height adjustment, zippered front pockets and ABS carry handles. It's all he can do to restrain himself when she sighs of duvet covers in cargo and camouflage, of curtains with new improved drape and liners to help save your furniture from damaging ultra-violet, of high performance ultra-sprung blown-cluster pillows full-corner filled with pre-sprung hollow polyester, extra-soft and flame retardant with a high support-rating and complimentary pillow protectors supplied.

He wants her beneath him now, so he can feel her breasts and look into her eyes and impress her tender skin with his stiff new Cougar motorcycle outfit (jumpsuit mode). It's time, in other words, to take charge of the situation. He stands and pulls her roughly/gently across to the dentist's chair, encourages her into it, knocks the seat's quick release with the reinforced gear-change toecap of his left black Belstaff Viper bootie and straight away is on top of her, all over her, rubbing and rocking and kissing. But throughout this and in spite of it she has remained attentive to detail and when tugged from the table had the presence of mind to tear several pages from out the catalogue and bring them with. What's more they're from *Ladieswear*, which is perfect.

She holds the rumpled sheets over his shoulder and reads them one by one before letting them fall singly onto the floor. *'The ruched top, because it's slinky, sexy and goes with everything,'* she tells him as he thrusts in like a piston. *'Breathable, luxurious and fully washable with the feel of heavyweight silk. Team the zip jacket with combat pants or shorts,'* she cajoles as he pushes deep inside. *'The ponyskin-look adds instant impact to simple modern shapes – and it feels great,'* she huffs, her toned pelvic floor muscles flexing round his backstroke. *'Latino style is big news this season – dramatic hemlines, hot prints and frills.'* These words forced out from her as he makes his final, determined, orgasmically targeted plunge.

The 3-in-1 TV! NICAM stereo for near-CD quality sound plus an illuminated clock and FM radio that'll wake you up in the morning or your choice of 3 wake-up tunes.

The catalogue model stares up, smiling cleanly, past our hero's Airdura®-encased neck and shoulder. Her gaze rests on the screen of the Goldstar® television hung from a ceiling bracket for the benefit of patients. Its screen acts as a mirror; in it she can see her own smile. Fixed in place around it, blending seamlessly with the professionally whitened teeth and the lips painted with Crystal Shimmer® plum lipgloss[29] from an unknown

29   Ingredients: polybutene, ppg-5, lanolin wax, petrolatum, lanolin oil, isoropyl palmitate, stearalkonium hectorite, candellila wax, propylparaben. may contain: iron oxides, titanium dioxide, d&c red #3 aluminium lake, d&c yellow #5 aluminium lake, mica carmine, manganese violet.

manufacturer, is a girl the world knows simply as Britney. Britney wears a Hot-crimson PVC jumpsuit, transparent belt in violet with flat 'donut' buckle and 'bondage' high-leg stretch stiletto boots (in crème; synthetic uppers). She is still dancing.

James Flint is author of *Habitus*. He was formerly an editor of *Wired UK* and is currently on sabbatical from his editorial post at *mute*. His forthcoming novel *button.com* is to be published this year.

speedo

Daren King

My dog's called Abscess. Means well but he stinks. Meant to be man's best friend. Fall down a mountain or manhole an' they bring you a barrel full of export beer. Ab ain't like that. If I died he wouldn't even turn up. Or he'd turn up late an' piss on me. Cock his leg an' grin. Eats me out of house an' home. Can't afford the rent as it is. Have to find some dozy cunt stupid enough to wanna share it. Stuck advert in the paper. Priced it way over the odds an put in black an' white that it's shit but London is so full of desperate cunts that findin' someone to share it will be a doddle. Whatever overpriced dump you advertise in London you get half a million wankers reply. One of 'em is sat right in front of me now. Pretty little bit of slit she is too. Might as well chat her up a bit. Then tell her to sling her hook.

"So what's your name then."

"Amy," she says smilin'. "What's yours."

"Don't answer me back. Who's interviewin' you 'ere, you or me. The name's Speedo. Speedo Nike. Rhymes with bike."

"Funny name."

"Is anyone laughin'."

"No."

"Then why did you say it's funny."

"I don't know."

"Do you know anythin'."

"Some things. I know what I like."

"What's that meant to mean."

"I'm not saying."

"Do you like dick."

139

"Sometimes."

"You'll like this one," I say holdin' my packet. "Fuckin' huge. Length of a football pitch. Fuckin' insane it is. Big slice of man meat. Are you hungry."

"No."

"Want a sandwich."

"No."

"How about some dick. Bend over an' I'll fuck you."

"No thanks."

"Then what the fuck are you 'ere for."

"I want to view the flat."

"I know that you daft cow. Let me ask you something. What do you do. For a livin'."

"I'm a student."

"O yeah. Still learnin' then are you. So you're a virgin then are you."

"No."

"You ain't a virgin."

"I'm not no."

"You have in the past received cock."

"So."

"The contract for this place states that as part payment for the rent you have to receive cock. Still interested."

"I am yes."

"Even though the contract says I get to fuck you."

"I need somewhere to live."

"How would you like me to strip you naked an'

pump you full of spunk."

"I don't know."

"Get your kit off and open your legs. Pump you so full of cream you'll think you're a cream cake." Daft cow thinks I'm serious. Maybe I am. Fuck knows. I stand up an start clearin' the table. Get rid of all this crap. Salt an' pepper shaped like a fat woman's tits. Squeezy ketchup bottle with more ketchup outside it than in it. Leftover takeaway. Chuck it all in the sink. "Come on then," I say. "Get naked an' get on the table. Pump you so hard you'll think you're a tyre."

"No."

"Fill you so full of sperm you'll think you're a sperm bank."

"I said no."

"Lick your arsehole till you think it's a second cunt. Alright Amy how about this. I get the dog. You get your kit off. Climb on the table. An' fuck the dog."

"No. No way."

"Don't decide yet. Wait till you see him. Cop a load of his balls." I leave her sittin' there an' go in my bedroom where Ab sleeps durin' the day. Pull off the duvet an' drag the lazy fuck onto the floor an' kick him around the room so he wakes up. What's that stink. Looks like he's left me a present. I scoop it up an' carry it to the kitchen an' dump it in his food bowl. He's yappin' round my legs pissin' me off. I turn to Amy an' clap my hands an' say: "You, naked, on the table, with the dog."

"No."

"Then get the fuck out of my flat."

"I want to see the bedroom."

"After I told you to fuck an animal. Alright, make a deal. If I show you the bedroom will you show me your cunt."

"I may do."

"Come 'ere then. You're in my room with me." Still stinks of dogshit from what Ab done in my bed. Not as bad as the kitchen though. This girl really is askin' for it. Might have to spank her. I sit on the bed an' watch her face as she checks out my stuff. Porn mag glued to the ceilin'. Sock so filthy it smells like a pair. Keep the burglars out. Lot of break-ins round 'ere. Gettin' trendy now, fuck knows why. "So what do you reckon."

"Where do I hang my dresses."

"Fuck your dresses. Stuff 'em under the bed. Walk round naked. Then people can fuck you whenever they like. I need eight references an show me your cunt."

She unbuttons her jeans an' takes 'em off an' lays on the bed pullin' her knickers to the side an' shows me her thatch. I climb on top for a closer look. Nice.

"Can I move in then."

"Let me see it held open. You wanted to see inside the flat didn't you. What if you come all this way an' I didn't open the front door. Open up an' you can move in."

"Like this."

"That's my girl. Hang on what you doin'." She's

pullin' my trousers down.

"Are you going to fuck me then Mister Nike."

"Er. Maybe later."

"What's the matter Mister Nike."

"Bit floppy as it goes. Knackered. Been workin' hard I 'ave. Ain't gay or nothin'."

"Do you find me intimidating Mister Nike."

"I think you better get out don't you."

"But Mister Nike – "

"Go on love, out you go." Got the door open, push her out in the street. Fuck. Not my type. "Come on Ab. You an me boy, upstairs."

Daren King is author of *Boxy an Star*, which was shortlisted for the 1999 Guardian First Book Award.